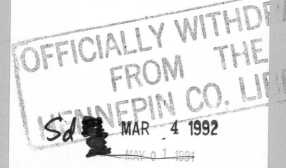

Rear-View Mirrors

By Paul Fleischman

Rear-View Mirrors

PAUL FLEISCHMAN

1 8 ◧ 1 7

————— HARPER & ROW, PUBLISHERS —————

Cambridge, Philadelphia, San Francisco, London, Mexico City, São Paolo, Singapore, Sydney

————— NEW YORK —————

Library of Congress Cataloging-in-Publication Data
Fleischman, Paul.
   Rear-view mirrors.

   "A Charlotte Zolotow book."
   Summary: When Olivia is summoned by her father, a
man she barely remembers, to determine whether she is
worthy of inheriting his legacy, she embarks on a
personal odyssey that teaches her the true meaning of
love and kinship.
   [1. Fathers and daughters—Fiction.
2. New Hampshire—Fiction] I. Title.
PZ7.F599233Re 1986   [Fic]   85-45387
ISBN 0-06-021866-5
ISBN 0-06-021867-3 (lib. bdg.)

for David Brooks
and
Jennifer Jany

Table of Contents

Rear-View Mirrors

1

Mailbox

I grew up acquainted with my father neither by sight nor by scent, but solely by report. He was like a distant land known only through travelers' tales, an inhospitable realm where strange and shocking customs survived. There, moths and butterflies were stalked, caught, dried, labeled, and displayed on the walls of every room, as if they were charms against evil spirits. Pea soup and bagels were the staple foods. The Boston Red Sox were noisily worshipped there and the tobacco leaf ritually burned, its foul-smelling smoke, unknown in our house, constantly rising upward like incense. My mother had been there, carrying me out of that country when I was eight months old. As my father, in the sixteen years after, hadn't found time to once call or write, I grew up to be grateful she'd taken me with her. She was his ex-wife; I was his ex-daughter.

I've found myself musing on all of this while making my way down Hatfield Road. I gaze out across the field to my left, hear a meadowlark singing, smell freshly cut hay, amazed by my present circumstances: to be strolling at dusk in North Hooton, New Hampshire, having started the day in Berkeley, California; to be in my father's town, walking down his road, heading intentionally toward his house, a destination I'd long vowed to avoid; to find the sight of the "Eggs" sign ahead and the row of sugar maples to my right not only familiar, but welcome. For this is my second trip here. My first was a year ago. In the interim, my father was killed by lightning while up on his roof, replacing shingles in a storm. I pass a beech tree, study the trunk, and remember what he said about beeches. The road is lined with such rear-view mirrors in which I behold the summer before. I round a curve, then pass by a mailbox—and at once think back a year, to his letter.

It was after my next-to-last day of eleventh grade that my mother came home from work and delivered it to me.

"Letter for Miss Tate!"

She announced this like a town crier, but seemed slightly anxious underneath her good cheer. I studied the envelope. It was addressed to me, in care of my mother, in care of the Sociology Department, University of California. In the corner was a return address in some town I'd never heard of in New Hampshire.

I peered down at the postmark, then up at my mother. "But I don't know a soul in New Hampshire."

"Been writing your address in telephone booths?" She fiddled nervously with an earring. " 'For a good read, write Olivia Tate, 1521 Cedar Street, Berkeley.' "

We both smiled. I thought about New Hampshire: maple syrup, snow in the winter, the first presidential primaries. But no one connected with the state came to mind.

"Olivia, dear—I've got a pile of papers on Lenin

3

I have to read after dinner. If you don't plan to open the letter by then, or want some *professional* help in reading it—"

I turned it over and slit it open. In the midst of which act I suddenly recalled hearing my mother speak of spending weekends, long ago, with my father at his parents' house, somewhere in New England.

I pulled out the contents of the envelope and felt my mother bending over my shoulder. In my hand I found an airline ticket, one way, in my name, from Oakland to Boston. Beneath it, a bus ticket from Boston to North Hooton, N.H. Under that, a handwritten note:

> Olivia,
>   Remarkable opportunity. Return trip paid. Come if you can.
>
> Your father

My mother seemed dazed. "My God," she murmured. "Truly remarkable."

I stared at the unfamiliar handwriting, reread the telegram-style message, and found an old Rolling Stones song playing in my head: "Under My Thumb." Which was where, it gradually dawned on me, I finally had my father. Begging two days. After I've done what I came here to do.

I close my eyes but they won't stay shut. My body knows it's not time for sleep. Suddenly, a whippoorwill starts singing, and my mind travels back to my first night here.

It was dark when the bus from Boston halted. The driver twisted around in his seat and smiled in my direction. "North Hooton!"

There was no place on earth I wanted to be less. I hauled down my mother's battered gray suitcase, wondering what I was doing here. She'd appeared to be proud of my resistance at first, then insisted I go and see my father. Perhaps because the chance might not come again. Or perhaps in hopes I wouldn't like what I saw, bearing out her leaving him in particular and her disappointment in men in general.

Reluctantly, I shuffled down the aisle. Back in Boston I'd thought about finding someone to use my bus ticket and name and letting my father, who wouldn't know the difference, take in a stranger for the summer. Descending the steps, I quickly realized that I couldn't be sure what he looked like either, since the few photographs we had of him were close to twenty years old.

I stepped out into the warm evening air—and froze at the sight of a man approaching. He had a newspaper in one hand and a cigarette in the other. His eyes looked me over, then lit at the sight of the white-haired woman exiting behind me. They kissed and walked off. The bus pulled away, leaving me alone at what seemed to be North Hooton's sole intersection.

I glanced around. I was in front of a café. The other three corners were occupied by a gas station, a post office, and a church—but no father. I leaned up against the streetlight behind me. There was no one about, no drivers slowed and stared, but I felt conspicuous just the same. And a fool for coming, when I could have passed out leaflets at a rent control rally that afternoon at which my mother was speaking. And when I could have had a paying job helping with the research for her articles, instead of wasting my time in Hicksville.

I stared up the street, looked at my watch, and wondered if the bus had been early. The mosquitoes were certainly there on time. I waved them away with my father's letter and speculated on his tracking us down. Our phone was unlisted. He didn't know our address. No problem

for the writer of a string of crappy mysteries star-
ring Virgil Stark, sonnet-writing private eye—
books I'd proudly refused to read. He probably
looked at a Berkeley catalog and found my mother
still on the faculty—the same job that had sprung
us free of him and New York City so long ago.
I smiled to imagine him seeing her now listed as
a full professor. And continued to smile at imagining his dilemma had her name not been there.

Ten minutes and a dozen mosquito bites later
I was ready to hitch back to Berkeley on the spot.
Then I realized I could try calling him from the
café, if *his* number wasn't unlisted. And if the
telephone had reached North Hooton. I picked
up my suitcase—then set it down at the sight of
a man coming down the steps.

He had a limp and a cane and was gesturing
toward me. He halted a moment and we stared
at each other. He was taller than my mother, as
was I. On his head was a ragged Red Sox cap.
In the light of the street lamp I gazed at his filthy
clothes and worn features and felt suddenly shaky.
Guilt-stricken, I studied his difficult walk, amazed
that I'd spent my life hating a cripple—then noticed my eyes were filling with tears, despite sixteen years of coaching to the contrary.

He approached, slowly, and peered into my face. Neither of us seemed to know what to say. Finally, he cleared his throat.

"If you're needing a lift somewhere, young lady—"

My jaw dropped. My eyes widened.

"No need to take offense!" He retreated a step. "Only trying to be neighborly!"

I gaped at the man. "You're not Hannibal Tate?"

His jaw dropped. He blinked. "No, ma'am."

I wiped away my wasted tears and hoped he hadn't noticed them.

"Floyd Peck. Live out on Hatfield Road, though. I drive right past Hal's, if that's where you're headed."

I nodded and found myself relieved to have regained a father I could safely despise. I picked up my suitcase and walked to his car, grateful for rural hospitality, wondering why my father hadn't picked up the trait. We set off and at once were surrounded by woods. I half-expected to see wolves in our headlights, to have our tires slashed by owls, our flesh fed to their young. I was soothed to hear my driver's voice, asking where I'd traveled from. And amused when my reply brought forth from him a summary of an article about some California feminists who'd lurked outside a liquor store, trailed home a man who'd bought a copy of *Playboy*, and left him hanging upside-down from a chandelier as a warning to others. Not wanting to disappoint him, I said it was true. He quickly declared that the only magazine he read was *American Dairyman*. I mentioned that some of the more radical bands had *talked* of targeting it as well. He slammed on the brakes. I thought I was going to be asked to walk the rest of the way there—but there was where we turned out to be.

"Looks like he's home," Mr. Peck spoke up cheerfully, anxious, it seemed, to be rid of me. Three lights were on in the house to our right. Vengefully, I pictured my father hanging by the ankles from one of them.

I retrieved my suitcase from the back seat of the car, thanked my chauffeur, and watched him drive off. Then I turned and stared at my father's house, reluctant to finally meet the man I'd traveled so many miles to see. The evening air felt foreign to me: hot and strangely heavy. I was sweating, though whether because of the heat or out of nervousness I wasn't sure. I stood for five minutes, then started up the driveway, not so much attracted by my father as repelled by the mosquitoes.

I climbed up the porch steps and set down my suitcase. I peered through the screen door into the living room, saw no one there, prepared to knock, then decided that that was too familiar a summons for someone who, until now, had wanted nothing to do with me, and who'd left me to wait at the bus stop besides. Taking great pleasure in treating him as the stranger he was, I rang the bell.

Footsteps sounded above. Stairs creaked. And it occurred to me that Mr. Peck might have pulled my leg as I had pulled his—and dropped me off in front of the wrong house. Which possibility, when a figure appeared, provided me with a justification for my stiffly formal greeting.

"Pardon me. But would you happen to be Mr. H. L. Tate?"

The man facing me was lit only from behind, reducing him to silhouette. "Yes, that's right."

I was thunderstruck. Wasn't he going to ask me in? Astounded, I stared at the shape before me: tall, broad-shouldered, holding a pipe. Surely he knew who I was. Or did women with suitcases commonly appear on his porch? I took a deep breath, determined not to lose this duel of indifference.

"Then I suppose it was you," I stated casually,

"who didn't meet me at the bus from Boston."

The shape took a step back and looked at its watch.

"My goodness—you must be Olivia."

I nodded.

"I forgot the time altogether."

I didn't believe him for a minute. The bastard! He'd swallowed his pride, sought me out, sent an invitation and a ticket—then turned the tables by not picking me up, forcing me to go hunting for him. Making *me* the seeker once again.

"I must have dozed off for an hour," he explained.

With a lit pipe in your mouth? I asked myself. Finally, he opened the door, and I picked up my suitcase and hauled it inside. A reunion several steps down from Stanley and Livingstone on the Great Meetings list.

"How did you get here?" my father asked.

I set down my things and turned around, seeing him for the first time in the light. And at once I felt my anger subside, overcome by the fascination of viewing my father in the flesh. Though at first sight he seemed more monument than man: massive frame, vast hands, giant feet. He was round-faced and bald, slightly flabby, and was dressed in an undershirt and checked shorts.

Each detail about him was a surprise, and my eyes flitted quickly from one to another: the bushiness of his graying eyebrows, his wire-rim glasses, the scar on one shin, the fineness of his fingers and their neatly trimmed nails. Then suddenly I recalled his question.

"A Mr. Peck drove me here," I replied. "He said he was going out this way."

My father thoughtfully sucked on his pipe. I noticed his eyes surveying me and couldn't help but wonder what he thought.

"Rather on the tall side, aren't you?" he inquired.

I was dumbstruck. Yes, I was tall. Too tall. *His* fault, it was now plain to see. I'd hoped for some fatherly compliment—and vowed not to let my defenses down again.

"I must say, your hair's darkened up a good deal." His voice was oversized and his cadence slow, as if he were an orator from the last century. "Despite all that surfing and lounging in the sun."

"There's no surfing on San Francisco Bay," I shot back.

He grunted. "And how's your mother faring? Still writing those pompous articles?"

I let this loaded question pass and noticed the

16

papers spread around his desk. "How's the Great American Novel coming?"

He continued as if I hadn't spoken. "I don't believe that woman could say 'Pass the salt' without footnotes to Aristotle, Karl Marx, Julia Child, and Amy Vanderbilt."

I waved away his vile-smelling smoke. "Is listening to *this* the 'remarkable opportunity' you dragged me here for?"

"The decision to come was yours," he replied. He blew a smoke ring into being and watched it jellyfish through the air. "As for the opportunity I mentioned, I can put it quite simply: I'm seeking an heir."

I cocked my head in surprise. "An *heir*?"

"I've led a solitary life," he announced. His manner was disinterested, businesslike. "George Washington, in his farewell address, warned the nation against 'entangling alliances.' I applied his advice to my personal life, and always found it to be sound counsel. Now, however, with my end drawing near, I've discovered myself desiring a successor. Someone to defend my reputation against critics and my grave against snowmobiles. To whom I could entrust the house and land, and the continuation of the Virgil Stark series." He walked to a window and gazed outside. "I felt I was bound to contact you first, as my only relation, aside from my brother. Though family blood counts for nothing in this. Should you prove unfit, or not want the position, I've a large pool of other applicants to draw from."

I studied my father in disbelief. "But your end's not drawing near—you're still young."

"Forty-nine, to be exact. And a recent sufferer of heart palpitations. Cardiac disease, it so happens, struck down both my father's parents."

"But even so—" I responded lamely. On the top shelf of the bookcase beside me I spotted a pair of cycling trophies, looked closer, and made out his name on both, struck that a former athlete should have so little confidence in his body.

"I suggest you give me, and New Hampshire, a month. After that, I'll pay your way back when you like." He turned around. "Have you eaten?"

"On the bus."

"Then you'll probably want to get some rest. Your room's upstairs, at the end of the hall."

He stood where he was, making no motion to help with my suitcase or show me the way.

"You may find it somewhat warm upstairs for sleeping, by California standards."

He smiled smugly. I thought of the heat in

Sacramento, my mother's hometown, and was about to speak up when he continued.

"Your mother whined constantly about the humidity. In light of which fact, and in spite of your sex's reputed edge in physical endurance, I've placed a small electric fan by your bed."

Some choice: I could either swelter or admit that my mother and I and all females were frail.

"Should you find it necessary," he added.

Lifting my suitcase, I tossed him a flat "Good night," marched up to my room, put the fan in the hall, and shut the door. It would just be four weeks, I reminded myself. Then he could sort through the rest of his "pool" of applicants—if they existed. Which, I mused while opening the windows, seemed highly doubtful. Which, in turn, explained the welcome I'd received, or the lack of it. For despite his unruffled, rhetorical style, my father was clearly desperate: sick with the fear of death, a disease for which I was his only known cure. His casual rudeness was merely a face-saving show of resistance to our new roles. He'd cast me aside; now he must court me.

Fanning myself with a magazine, I turned a circle in the center of the room. It was small and low-ceilinged, containing a bed, night table, rocking chair, bookcase, and chest. On one wall was a frame holding two amber moths. I approached and read the label beneath them: "Huckleberry Sphinx." I went to the bathroom, nearly falling over the fan when I walked out the door. Then I got my nightgown out of my suitcase, slipped it on in the dark, and lay down. Two minutes later I took it off. Two minutes after that I noticed I was starting to think about the fan, then clenched my teeth and struggled to forget it. I was slippery with sweat. Mosquitoes whined in my ears. No hint of a breeze entered the windows, just the racket of crickets and frogs and God-knew-what-other natural insomniacs. I felt as if I was on the set of *Tarzan*, not snug in some quaint New England village, and wondered if I'd be dead of malaria by the time my month here finally ended. I tried to put myself to sleep by fantasizing my return to California: kissing the concrete at the Oakland airport, inhaling the salt air, rejoicing in the fog, pledging my allegiance to the Golden Gate—then was interrupted by the call of a bird.

It was simple and clear and very close by: three notes repeated over and over. It was new to me, and seemed strangely sad. Abruptly, the singing stopped, though the song continued to sound in my head. And suddenly I remembered my mother's recollection, on the way to the airport, of listening to this very bird's call her first night in the East—and sat up in bed, wide awake, realizing I too had just heard my first whippoorwill.

3

Butterflies

The sun rises, stares me straight in the eye, and I grope for my watch on the table. It reads 5:15, but my body is still in California and feels strongly that the sky should be black, the birds silent, and sensible people asleep in their beds. I get up from mine, put on T-shirt and shorts, and search my backpack for the New Hampshire map. I take out the bag of granola as well, and admire the pack a moment: it's new, bought with the money I earned this year, a step up from my mother's hand-me-down suitcase. Then I go downstairs, case the kitchen, and give thanks to my uncle when I find some canned milk. I decide that if I choose to live here when the house becomes mine on my twenty-first birthday, I'll always keep a six-pack of his beloved Bluebird ale on hand.

I take my bowl of granola outside and sit in the sun on the porch steps. The air is cool. Spiderwebs are still dewed. Swallows are swooping around the barn. I unfold the map, locate North Hooton, then spot Lake Kiskadee to the north. I wonder how the ride came to be an annual tradition for my father and am startled to measure it for the first time and find that it's nearly a seventy-mile loop. Longer, I reflect, than the trip across my high school stage at graduation last week—but otherwise so similar. I recall my mother standing when my name was announced and clapping conspicuously, despite which spectacle I managed, somehow, not to trip on my robe. I'd always been a good student, had earned straight As that semester, and graduated with honors. She was proud of me; by her standards I'd succeeded and was now, in her eyes, an adult. But for me the ceremony felt incomplete. Which is why I stopped here on the way to Maine: to perform a corresponding rite of passage in the imagined presence of my father. To attempt the ride

23

he took each year. To acknowledge his influence and picture his approval. To graduate in his eyes.

I take in my bowl, find a grocery bag, and put in it my wallet and knife and some food. I fill my canteen and put it in too. Then I comb my hair— I've let it grow out since last summer, till it now almost reaches my waist—braid it to keep it out of my face, put on a cap, and lock the house behind me. A swallow flies out the barn door when I open it. I wheel out the bike and clean off the seat. It's an old Raleigh ten-speed, forest green under the dust, with a small wicker basket in the front. Not likely to be seen in the Olympics, but it'll do for me, as it did for my father. I close the barn door, put my bag of supplies in the basket, and straddle the bike. I pause. Then I raise the creaking kickstand with my foot. And suddenly I'm off.

I slither down the dirt drive, turn onto the harder-packed dirt of Hatfield Road, and find out at once that the seat is too high. My feet can barely stay with the pedals—not surprising, given my father's height. I figure that I can put up with it till the gas station, then start up a rise. I reach for the changer and shift down two gears, relieved to learn that the derailleur works. I pass the Rabbs' house. The road turns to pavement and the air is suddenly sweet with hay. I hear chickadees calling and see what I think might be a chestnut-sided warbler. Then I coast down a hill, the cool air raising goosebumps, spot the white spire of the Congregational church, turn right, and pull in at the gas station.

The "Closed" sign is up. It doesn't open till seven. I look at my watch, find it's only 6:20—then hear what sounds like a tool falling. I walk around to the side of the station and am surprised to see the garage door open, a car inside, and a pair of black sneakers sticking out from under it.

"Excuse me, but can I fill up my tires?"

A body slides out from beneath the car and I'm further amazed to find that it's Owen's.

"Olivia! How do you like that."

This, I note to myself, is one of his longer speeches on record. I smile. "Didn't think I'd run into you here," I state truthfully. "But I'm glad I did." Also true.

"Just fixing my car. Before I start on other people's." He stands up, as tall as I am now, and seems pleased to see me. A great relief, since I'm much in his debt, unknown to him.

"I've got the carving on my dresser at home," I say, repaying part of it.

Modestly, he shrugs this off, wiping his greasy

25

hands with a rag. "Sorry about your dad last fall."

"Ancient history," I answer him, shrugging off his statement in return. We catch up on the past twelve months and trade fall plans: U.C.L.A. for me, building cabinets in his uncle's shop for him. He fills my tires till they're hard as granite, checks my chain, and gives it some oil. Then, even though I can do it myself, I let him lower the seat a few inches, perhaps to provide further cause to thank him. Which I do several times, explain I have to go, and promise I'll write him about the dig.

I ride half a block to Danforth's Grocery, take a newspaper from the pile by the door, and leave a pair of dimes in payment. I open it up to the weather, find there's a chance of showers, then spot what I'm after: "Sunset: 8:30 P.M."

I stuff the newspaper into my basket and glance at my watch. It's 6:45. Which leaves me something more than thirteen hours. For the point of the ride, my father made clear, wasn't simply to view the scenery along Highways 30, 14, and 520—but to make it back home before the sun went down. An odd condition, like the wearing of gowns and mortarboards at graduation. But one I've sworn myself to meet.

I return to the crossroads, head north, and soon

am informed that I'm leaving the village of North Hooton. After which I start up my first real hill, wondering—since I'm no marathon biker—why I didn't look at a map, see that the ride would be seventy miles long, and train for it back in California. Panting, I reply reasonably enough that I assumed I could easily pedal as far as a fifty-year-old with heart palpitations. And all of a sudden, as I crest the hill, my father's motive in taking this trip is revealed to me: it's no sight-seeing tour, but a race, against the coming of night. A race he must have relished last summer, performed during one of those occasional spells when his surrender to hypochondria was replaced by a passion for besting Death. The same mood of defiance, no doubt, that led him up to his roof in a thunderstorm.

I shift gears, pass a cornfield on my left, and gradually regain my breath. Then I'm jolted by the thought that, just like my father, I'm using this trip to resist his mortality. Resurrecting him by reenacting his ride, taking his Raleigh over his old route as if to maintain the illusion of his living. The notion stuns me. I wonder if it's true. Then two butterflies flit in front of me, and as if I'm on Eastern Variable Time, my mind at once jumps back a year.

* * *

"Butterflies are lured to nectar, men to butterflies."

I turned from the mounted pair I'd been eying and beheld my father coming downstairs. It was late in the morning, my first in North Hooton. Out of foolish politeness I'd held back from eating breakfast alone and was famished.

"I see that you too are a lover of the order Lepidoptera," he proclaimed.

"Actually, what I'd love even more at the moment is some food."

"And who could resist," he continued, approaching the butterflies, "the alluring sight of one of nature's most flighty and ephemeral creatures preserved behind glass, fixed in space and immune to the passage of time."

Was this, I asked myself, the explanation for his ardor for them: not as insects to be appreciated in the field, but as symbols of eternal life, poised permanently in midflight on his walls?

"Shall we grab a net and collecting jar and see what we can find fluttering about?"

I rolled my eyes at his wishful presumption that I shared his obsession. "Maybe later. I'm starved."

"Starved! Is that all you can say this morning?"

He stepped back and glared at me with contempt. "I perceive distinct signs of Dr. Spock's second edition in your upbringing. Feeding on demand!" He sneered at the notion and entered the kitchen. "Or did your mother prefer Machiavelli's *The Prince* for guidance in raising a grasping child?"

I charged after him. "And where were you with your expert advice on childrearing?"

He closed a cupboard and turned to face me. "You don't know how *lucky* you are I wasn't there. I wasn't meant for marriage, and certainly not for raising children. No more than were my parents." He gestured toward a framed photograph on the wall. "As they demonstrated in the naming of their offspring."

I glanced from their faces to his. "Why 'Hannibal'?"

"They were both professors of history. Collaborating, at the time of my birth, on a book on the Roman Empire. A project they felt, no doubt rightly, that I threatened."

I looked back at his parents, both smiling warmly, and wondered how they could have done such a thing.

"My brother Leo's full name is Napoleon. Born just as they were starting their study of Russia." He took out a bag of bagels from the refrigerator, then gave me a basket. "Speaking of which, go out to the barn and see if socialism is still intact and each hen giving according to her ability."

I walked outside and over to the barn, realizing I'd never been in one before. Cautiously, I opened the door and was greeted with soft, suspicious cackling. I stepped into the gloom. Suddenly I made out a goat to my left, instantly froze, then discovered with relief that it was penned. To my right was a waist-high row of nesting boxes. The half dozen hens occupying them muttered conspiratorily as I poked around in search of eggs. I didn't find any and was about to leave—then it dawned on me that they were under the hens. Not chancing to be dressed in armor, I ruled out reaching my bare hand underneath. Then I noticed a rake, picked it up, positioned myself at a respectful distance, and gently budged a hen off her nest. She burst into flight. I crept forward, brandishing the rake in defense, and found two brown eggs. Placing them proudly in my basket, I retreated, held out the rake, and proceeded to bulldoze the lot of them off their nests. With hens flying and squawking and scuttling, I hurried down the row, snatched up six more eggs, headed gratefully for the door—and slid three feet on a pile of droppings, launching my harvest into orbit before I fell.

Eggs splatted all over the floor of the barn. I slowly picked myself up from the straw and manure, feeling fouled for life, and looked in the basket. Two eggs remained. I cursed the chickens, all cackling merrily, cleaned myself off with a rag, then wondered if my father might be coming to investigate. Fearfully, I grabbed a shovel, scooped up the wreckage of shells and yolks, and dumped the slimy mess in the goat's pen, praying that goats ate eggs. This one did.

I picked up the basket and straightened my hair, tried to seem calm, strode out the barn door as if I'd just graduated from charm school—and nearly had a head-on with my father, who was carrying an old soup kettle.

"How many this morning?"

I showed him the basket.

"Two eggs?"

I nodded.

"I need *six* to make omelets. And as your mother and all good revolutionaries know, you can't make an omelet without cracking eggs." He turned toward the hens. "Or without *laying* them."

He entered the goat's pen, tied her neck to a

post with a rope, and began milking her.

"Ever taste goat's milk?"

"A few times," I lied. I watched him shoot it into the kettle, studied the goat's strange coffee-colored eyes, then gaped at the sight of bits of shell on her chin.

"Is that all you've got?" my father asked her, peering into the kettle.

I considered brushing off her chin myself, but didn't feel like finding out firsthand whether or not goats bite.

"You can forget about that two-week vacation on the shores of the Black Sea," he informed her. He gave a few final squeezes, untied the goat, and, to my relief, left the pen. "And Lenin aside," he boomed to the barn at large, "there won't be any 'withering away of the state' whatsoever around here. Not until milk and egg yields go up!" A comment, like so many others, mocking my mother—and indirectly me.

We returned to the house and finally had breakfast, during which I took my first sip of goat's milk. And last—I spit it all over my plate. It may have been country fresh, but it tasted to me like it had sat in the sun for three months.

"Now for our stroll through the field," said my father.

I felt like I'd already had more than enough of Mother Nature that morning. But what else was there to do in this wasteland? He fetched a butterfly net, handed me a jar, and we set off out the back door.

"Those are red pines you see at the edge of the field," he proudly declared. Not that I'd asked. "I tended that grove on weekends as a boy."

I could think of better things to do with a weekend.

"That tree you see over there is a beech." He pointed as we wandered through the long grass. "Smooth gray bark. Leaves yellow in the fall. Muscular trunks—always make me think of the human limbs Michelangelo drew."

He paused to admire the tree a moment and I suddenly saw what he wanted in an heir. Someone to whom he could leave not simply his house and land but, more important, his loves: for his pines, for beech trunks, for butterflies. A successor who, far in the future, would take his own grandchildren on this same walk, view the same tree, and speak of Michelangelo. Someone through whom his enthusiasms would survive.

"The white flower to your left is Queen Anne's lace."

I glanced at it out of duty, then spied a shiny

black stone and picked it up. I'd collected rocks ever since I could remember—they were the only part of nature that roused me—and I brushed this one off and tucked it in my pocket.

"Though in Berkeley's botanical gardens," he went on, "where anti-royalist feeling runs high, you'd be prudent to use the plant's more humble alternate name—wild carrot."

I raised my hand to fight off the sun. An action that, in that humid air, was enough to make my body burst into sweat.

"That's milkweed to the right. The monarch butterfly's favorite."

I unstuck my hair from my sweat-slick neck, wondered if it might mildew on me, then felt a mosquito bite my thigh. "Is that all there is to do around here—memorize the names of flowers all day?"

My father resumed walking, unperturbed. "He who tires of North Hooton," he bellowed theatrically, "tires of life." He crouched and stared at a caterpillar. "Your mother never cared for the country either, despite females' famous kinship with the earth." He straightened up with a sigh and moved on. "I believe her knowledge of nature has been gained entirely by the study of woodland scenes on maple syrup containers."

"She knows whippoorwills," I spoke up in her defense.

"God help her if she doesn't! That's one bird that *tells* you its name every time it calls." He examined a beetle, then proceeded onward, his muslin net slung over his shoulder. "Her idea of a hike was a walk through the Bowery, where the wildlife was largely beggars and drunks. Though I suppose she may have produced, unknown to me, a learned tract or two on the life of that city-loving bird, the starling." He halted. " 'The Avian Proletariat: Starling Population Growth, as Predicted in Marx's Ornithological Writings.' "

I was racking my brains for a retort when he peered at a flower, then swooped down upon it with his net.

"Banded hairstreak," he announced with pleasure. He took the jar I'd been holding, transferred his catch to it, and held it up. "Now tell me that isn't a beautiful sight."

"Right up there with the *Mona Lisa*," I answered with a maximum of apathy. The butterfly was tiny and brown and wasn't fluttering about at all. "What's the white stuff in the bottom of the jar?"

"Plaster of paris, on top of potassium cyanide

crystals. The fumes kill them quickly, with almost no damage to—"

"Yoo-hoo! Bull!"

We both spun around to find a gnomish figure topped with a bonnet bearing toward us. My father's face fell.

"Oh, Christ—not her."

The woman was wearing boots and a long crimson skirt, which she lifted above the grass.

"Such a glorious day!" she erupted as she reached us. "Straight out of van Gogh, wouldn't you say, Bull?" She smiled up at him sweetly, then cast a worried glance at me. "Who's your friend?"

"That's my daughter Olivia. Here for a visit."

The woman seemed greatly relieved by this answer. My father gestured toward her with his net. "Flora Gill. Famous painter and professor of art at Oakes College, up the road in Ashton."

" 'Famous'—how could you!"

His duty disposed of, my father resumed stalking butterflies.

"I'm sure your daughter's never heard my name."

Nor had I ever heard anyone call him "Bull" or imagine I'd ever be regarded as a rival for his affections.

"Of course," she confided in me, "the name van Gogh was unknown when he died. Utterly!" She smiled with satisfaction at the thought, loosening the makeup over her wrinkles. "Emily Dickinson? The very same story. And Mozart— buried in an unmarked grave!"

My father brought down his net, then swore. All three of us watched his quarry flutter off.

"The freedom of flying things never ceases to move us, does it?" Flora put forward.

My father sneered at this proposition.

"A living metaphor for the soul, do you think?" she suggested as we strolled along.

My father's eyes rolled. Then he sighted something, stopped us, and crept on ahead alone.

"I certainly hope he's not after one of those giant, gaudy butterflies." She untied the yellow ribbon holding down her bonnet, took it off, and fanned herself with it. "I can't look at that kind without thinking of Graham."

I defended myself against a cloud of gnats and wondered when nature class would be over. "Who's that?"

"Graham Gill, my former husband. I'm sure you must have heard of *him*." Her voice was sharp with resentment of this fact. "His paintings, geared to the popular taste, began to sell for five figures, then six. There were interviewers waiting at the door, retrospectives, fast cars, fancy clothes—while no one in New York would hang my work."

Eying her lipstick, which looked as if it had been put on by Jackson Pollock, I had no trouble believing in her failure.

She smirked knowingly. "Of course, in the world of art, as in heaven, the last shall be first—something Graham never understood. I can't tell you what a relief it was to leave both him and New York behind, to be free of the commercial distractions that have corrupted so many talents in the past." My father returned and she took his arm. "To share the company of *genuine* artists, undefiled by success—like your father."

His eyes bulged. "As it happens, I've only just heard that *Virgil Stark and the Walden Pond Murders* is going into its seventh printing."

I noticed Flora's smile wilt.

"Really," she replied, as if some disaster had been reported. She glanced at her watch. "My, the morning. I only intended to stay long enough to invite you to brunch on Sunday. Both of you, naturally." She beamed at my father. "Afterward, Bull, perhaps you'll have time to sit for the portrait."

My father's face stiffened. "Actually, Olivia and

I have a rather full schedule on Sunday."

What, I wondered, could a full schedule consist of in this land of boredom?

"Well, do *try*," Flora pleaded, walking off.

"Not on your life," my father muttered. He marched ahead in a new direction. Wearily, I trailed behind.

"She's been nagging me over that portrait for months. No doubt she wants it for a voodoo image. Not to kill me, but worse—to lead me to the altar."

Sweat-soaked and scratched and bug-bit, I found myself comforted by the thought of a cool, dark church. Preferably air-conditioned.

"That woman's driving ambition in life is to be buried in a pauper's grave. But she's not going to drag *me* into it." He studied a stand of flowers before him. "I lied about the book I mentioned— it's just gone out of print this year. How I'd love to be defiled by fame! I don't *want* to be one of those inconspicuous butterflies she prizes. Gotcha!"

He brought down his net, his face fierce as a samurai's. "Brown elfin. Just the sort she adores!" And as if performing voodoo himself, he coaxed it into the killing jar, grinned vengefully, and screwed down the lid.

39

4

Pie Tin

The sun is finally high enough so that the brim of my cap keeps it out of my eyes. I look at my watch. It's just after nine. I know that I've been making good time, and swoop down a hill like a hawk on a dive. A dog tears down his driveway after me, but I easily outrace him.

I glide alongside a lake. A few ghostlike wisps of mist are still rising from it, and I smile, supremely happy to be here. The sight of swamp maples, the scent of the hayfield to my left, the phoebe's song I hear are all familiar, like old friends at the door. I'm surprised at how good it feels to be among them again, to have a second home. And pleased that the prospect of spending the day by myself seems attractive: a change for me.

I pass a row of summer cabins and breathe in the smell of breakfast being cooked. Watching a man row two children on the lake, I feel proud to have planned and paid for this return trip east entirely on my own—then hear the rumble of a truck behind me. It sounds big. The road is narrow and I quickly move as far to the right as I can. Just as it's rushing past I spot a pothole directly in front of me. There's no time to react, no chance to prepare. My front wheel sinks, whips right, and I fly forward through space like a weightless astronaut. And come quickly to earth on my right elbow and leg, the sound of which impact is drowned out even in my own ears by the roar of the truck.

Its noise subsides; my body's emerges. My arm and knee are both screaming for help. I look behind me and see that my bike is sprawled halfway into the lane. As if reliving my infancy, I struggle onto all fours, bring one leg up, slowly unbend the other, limp over to the bike, and drag it out of the road. I squat beside it, close my eyes, and rest, waiting for my heart to quit pounding. Then

I straighten up and check myself over.

My right elbow feels like it's been sledgehammered out of shape. Slowly, I flex my arm a few times, wondering if I'll ever play Frisbee again. I've got gory, Hollywood scrapes on my right knee and thigh—except that this is blood and not catsup. I hunt for something to clean them with, can't find anything suitable, and consider going back to one of the cabins for help. Then I think of my father's New England independence, determine to make do on my own, as he would, and settle for a page of the newspaper I bought. I spit on it, for what reason I'm not sure, wipe the scrapes, and wince at the sting. And marvel that I could have praised myself as a planner just moments before. Why didn't I bring a first-aid kit along? I gape at the Raleigh. And what about tools? Fearfully, I pick up the bike, straighten the basket, and walk it a few feet. The back wheel makes its familiar clicking. I don't see anything broken. It seems to be fine. As am I, I come to realize. I drink some water, stroll a few yards, and finally feel ready to ride. I put my canteen back in the basket. Then I lift my leg gingerly over the bar and set off at a gentle pace.

My scrapes stretch and burn with every pump. My knee is sore. Nevertheless, I give thanks that

I didn't hit my head on the asphalt. Then I notice my front wheel rubbing the brakes and my mood of gratitude vanishes. I lean forward and study the wheel while I ride. It's no longer perfectly round, but has a slight dent that scrapes the brakes each time around. I try opening the brakes wider, without success, and wonder if the problem is serious. With no alternative but to hope that it isn't, I pedal to Finchley and open my map, turn onto Highway 14, heading east, wind alongside a stream for several miles, then pull off the road for a midmorning snack.

I lean the bike up against a tree. Taking my food bag out of the basket, I realize I didn't even glance at the headlines of the paper I bought, grab it as well, and sit back against a boulder. I scan the front page while eating an apple, recalling my father's disdain for the news, his unshakable disinterest in the world. I quickly flip through the rest of the paper, aware of the fact that I now merely skim stories I would have once dissected, but confident I'll never descend to his appalling level of apathy.

A band of blue jays screams by overhead. I inspect my wounds, decide to donate my apple core to the local fauna, and manage to toss it only ten feet on account of my aching elbow. Still hungry, I open my bag of dates. I pop one in my mouth, survey the stream below, sequined by the morning sun, then reach for a stone that catches my eye. Something I've done thousands of times, without understanding or wondering why. Yet this time my mind examines the act, my eyes watch my hand pick it up—a deed that seems to take place in slow motion—and I'm suddenly filled with the certainty that I'm lured to rocks not by their beauty but rather by their great age, by their link to former eras, buried cultures, dimly pictured ancestors. Absently, I stare at the stone, then am struck by the suspicion that this pull toward the veiled past has its source in a quest for knowledge of a very recent ancestor, yet one mysterious as Peking Man: my father.

Dazed by the thought, I roll the stone in my palm. Then I notice that one of its faces looks chipped and wonder whether human hands shaped it. Gazing before me, I begin to imagine a Stone Age hunting camp down by the stream. This reconstruction of the past from an artifact, of the whole from a part, I find pure joy. Or, more precisely, ninety-nine percent joy, one percent guilt. I muse on that other ancestor, my mother, who always seemed baffled by my collecting rocks, who never encouraged me in that pursuit, and yet who, in the past twelve months, has accepted my leap into archaeology without a word of criticism. I feel sure she wishes I were back passing out leaflets with her, researching her articles, engrossed in the issues of the present, not the Ice Age. And I feel indebted to her for not showing it. Maybe she was steeled for such a shift all along.

I pack up my food, put the stone in my pocket, and walk the Raleigh back to the road. I get on and push off, in the midst of which act I catch sight of the glint from an aluminum pie tin lying among the weeds. A bit of litter that I recognize as an artifact from my own history—around which my memory at once reconstructs a July morning from the summer before.

"Yours," boomed my father, "is a sweet-tempered ocean."

His voice rose above the crash of the waves, as if he were a Biblical prophet preaching to the whitecaps and seagulls and stones.

"Ours," he continued, "is a wrathful one."

I peered out at the Atlantic, my first view of it, and the first time I'd realized New Hampshire had a coastline. The water struck me as strangely green.

"A fearsome ocean," he boasted. "Ruled by Jehovah, not Jesus—or Frankie Avalon." He locked the car, picked up the picnic basket, and led the way to the beach.

"We've got storms on the Pacific too," I spoke up.

He ignored me.

"And sharks. And killer whales."

He spread out a blanket and unpacked our breakfast of bagels, oranges, cheese, and hot coffee. The sky was blue and the breeze stiff, adding sand to the menu. Despite which, it felt great to be by the ocean, even if it wasn't the one I'd have preferred.

"Lobster boat." My father pointed. "Best lobsters in the world come from New England." He poured himself some coffee and eyed me. "Though since you grew up in vegetarian Berkeley, and would have had to cross the county line to legally dine on meat or fish, I don't suppose you're impressed."

"You're right, I'm not." I struggled to remember if I'd ever actually tasted lobster.

"Nor, I suppose, should I expect you to care that Plymouth Rock is just down the coast. That America's roots, and your own, begin here."

I reached over, picked up an orange, and peeled

it onto this sacred ground. "So how many Russian Jews were on the *Mayflower*?"

"That was your *mother's* family!" he shouted. "The Tates have been here since 1640, and took a leading part in colonial affairs."

I waved off a fly. "The Salem witch trials, for instance?"

"As it happens, there were a few lawyers among them. Whose descendents might possibly have prosecuted your mother's anarchist ancestors."

"They were *unionizers*—not anarchists!"

"From whom she no doubt inherited her tendency to join groups."

I spit out a pair of orange seeds. It was true she was always going to meetings, making phone calls, starting committees having to do with one cause or another. But how else could you change things?

"Never," my father went on, "have I seen a calendar as crammed as hers. I always suspected she suffered from a fear of her own unreality. Causing her to live by the creed 'I make appointments, therefore I am.' "

"And what do you do with your free time? Chase *butterflies* while the world goes to hell!"

He leaned back on his elbows. "And why shouldn't I? The world is here to be enjoyed.

There are plenty of others who'll see to its saving, who take the same pleasure in that that I take in netting a spicebush swallowtail. Thank God such people exist—though I found it irksome to be married to one of them. Something you might want to keep in mind."

"I'll do that," I said with a smirk. "I promise I'll never marry a butterfly fanatic." Not that I had any thoughts of getting married—I still hadn't had a boyfriend, and wasn't overly troubled by the fact. My mother had concluded that men weren't worth the bother; I was too tall, too plain-faced, and too busy with her political endeavors to have disputed her finding. She'd always seemed pleased that I wasn't one of those girls who spend hours in front of the mirror, and I felt proud to be taking petitions around and reading Gandhi and tacking up fliers while the rest of my classmates sat in movies with dates.

"I *am* grateful she introduced me to bagels," my father said, slicing one in half.

Instantly, I missed her and the breakfasts she made us both in the mornings—missed her as if I were six years old and had never been away from home before.

"Lest you think," he continued, "I've got nothing good to say about her."

The meaning of the phrase "left-handed compliment" suddenly became clear to me.

"Do you suppose she'll ever marry again?"

I stretched out and buried my feet in the sand. "I think you broke her of the habit."

"She'd have to get hold of someone," he continued, paying no attention to me, "who wouldn't object to discovering Sacco's and Vanzetti's birthdays written in on the calendar but not his own."

"They happened to be great men," I shot back, defending both my mother and them.

"Then I'm afraid you'll be shocked to find that the celebration of their births has fallen into sad neglect of late in North Hooton." He sipped his coffee, viewing the waves. "Last year the stores kept regular hours. And this year there's even talk of mail delivery."

I ignored him, attending instead to a sea gull diving into the sea for a fish.

"You'd have thought your mother regarded herself as married, in spirit, to that pair of martyrs—the way nuns are said to be brides of Christ." My father smiled at the thought. "Then again, I suppose by now she's jumped on the feminist bandwagon and sworn off the male sex. I've read that some women are even researching doing away with men altogether and continuing the species on their own."

"Better living through chemistry, as they say."

"I hear that they're going back to their Bibles." His voice had a matter-of-factness to it that warned me he was pulling my leg. "That they're studying up on the virgin birth. And that the pet shops can't meet the demand for doves."

I reached for a bagel and bit into it. "I'll keep it in mind for my science fair project."

"Just this last week I read a review of a book claiming that God is a woman."

"Judging by the screwed-up state of the world, I've never had trouble believing he's male."

"The next thing women will want," he continued, "is to break into major league baseball!" An outrage he apparently found even more shocking than seizing the throne of God.

We finished eating, packed up our basket, and I wrote my mother a long letter. Afterward, we strolled for an hour along the beach, a heaping handful of whose stones I stuffed in my pockets. Then we started back toward home. In the course of which forty-five-minute drive, my father discoursed, in tour-guide fashion, on the magnificence of his state's salt marshes, the exquisite practicality of her stone fences, the perfection of her climate, the charm of covered bridges, and the advantages of attending a small college, of which New Hampshire boasted many. A sales pitch that impressed me not with the Granite State, but with his desperation.

We turned onto Hatfield Road, passed our house, and drove on to that of Mr. Peck, the man who'd given me a lift to my father's the night I'd arrived in North Hooton. We found him in the barn, peering into a cow's ear.

"Morning, Floyd," my father said. "I was wondering if you could spare us some straw. We're going to be mulching the garden today."

I didn't care for his use of the word "we"— especially since I'd never heard the word "mulching." Nor did I care for the dozen cows looking me over as if I might be lunch. Some of their backs were nearly up to my chin, and I was glad to see they were confined in their stalls.

Mr. Peck grabbed his cane and hobbled across the barn. On one wall of which I spotted a bumper sticker: "U.S. Out of the U.N." Presumably placed there for the benefit of his cows.

"I read where they had another earthquake in California," he said, eying me.

My father didn't subscribe to a paper, but I watched the news each night on TV, alone, and had heard a quick mention of it. And had noticed a relish in the reporter's voice, as if California were being punished for its sins.

"Ten injured," Mr. Peck continued. He pointed to a stack of bales of straw. My father paid him for two, placed one in my arms, and hoisted up the second. Trailing Mr. Peck, we trudged back to the car.

"Two million dollars' damage!" he crowed. Then he turned toward me, his face pale, fearful perhaps that, being a Californian, I'd bring down a similar calamity on North Hooton.

We put the bales in the trunk and headed home. Mr. Peck tipped his Red Sox cap. I suspected he hoped we wouldn't stop until I'd been safely returned to the Pacific. Instead, my father turned up our driveway, waved to a gangly boy mowing our lawn, and drove on to the garden, behind the barn.

"Who's that?" I asked him.

"Owen Pearce. Lives half a mile up the road." We lifted the bales out of the trunk. "Helps out with the heavier yardwork most weekends. Given the sorry state of my heart."

He entered the barn and returned with a knife and a transistor radio, snipping the bailing twine with one and tuning in the Red Sox game with the other. Then he stood a moment and surveyed his plot.

"Tending the garden," he proudly proclaimed, "is a venerable New England tradition."

I wasn't aware that New England had a monopoly on that particular custom. And I doubted the Puritan fathers would have approved of their hallowed rite being performed to the racket of the radio.

"The garden is a living symbol of renewal." My father strolled down a row of potatoes like a general reviewing his troops. "And spreading a mulch at the base of the plants, keeping out weeds and keeping in moisture, is a vital part of its maintenance."

He walked back toward a bale and grabbed a handful of straw.

"Your mother, no doubt, holds Aristotle's view that man is a political animal." He packed the straw around a pepper plant. "Today we'll confirm the definition I prefer: Man is the only animal that mulches."

Contemplating the garden's great size, I wasn't sure that I wanted to fully realize my human potential and spread straw around every one of its plants. It was an ark of vegetables, with every sort, from asparagus to zucchini, represented.

What exactly my father would do with it all when it ripened I'd no idea—unless gorging hourly on salads was an old New England tradition too.

"My parents," he bellowed above the radio, "had their garden right here as well. I still recall helping them as a boy."

He was working among the cucumbers. Reluctantly, I took up an armful of straw and started in on the onions.

"*Every* New England child learns to garden. In this part of the country we guide our steps by the light of the Bible and the Burpee seed catalog." He stopped and wiped his glasses with a handkerchief. "Many winter nights I've found spiritual strength in the pages of the Burpee catalog—consoling myself with its promise of spring. And the Bible, of course, as I'm sure you're aware, is a treasure trove of gardening advice. How to deal with plagues of locusts, and so on. . . ."

I was too intent on getting the chore done and myself out of the sun to smile. After half an hour of crawling down rows, listening to gardening lore with one ear and trying to tune out the Red Sox with the other, I stood up, wiped my brow, and found that we'd finished.

"You can report to your mother," my father

announced, admiring our labors, "that I've freed my serfs. And that I'm working my fields, my pores producing the honest sweat of the working class."

My brain was too hot to think up a reply. I lay back in a strip of shade by the car. And was at once disheartened by the sight of my father emerging from the barn with an armload of stakes from which pie tins fluttered on strings.

"Next, we'll pound these into the ground."

At which point it became quite clear to me why most people simply went to the store when they wanted some vegetables.

"To help keep the birds and rabbits away." He dropped several stakes and a hammer beside me. "They say their flashing in the sun scares them off."

I got up and started pounding them in, lest I bring on a comparison of western loafing and eastern industry.

"Anything else you want, Mr. Tate?"

I turned around and saw that the boy who'd been mowing the lawn had joined us.

"Just one thing." My father smiled. "I'd like you to meet my daughter Olivia."

The boy looked my way. He was dark-haired

and bony. I kept on hammering away at my stake.

"Owen," my father addressed me, "will be a senior in the fall, like yourself."

I gave a brief smile. Out of habit I quickly compared our heights and saw I was taller, though only by an inch or two.

"Olivia's from California."

Owen nodded impassively.

"From near San Francisco," my father added. I'd heard that New Englanders were known for not talking much and had the distinct feeling my father was struggling to get him to speak.

"Ricky asked if he can do the yardwork next week as usual, or if you want me again."

My father's face fell. Those weren't the words he wanted—and suddenly I understood why.

"I'll—let you know," he fumbled in reply. He pulled out his wallet and paid Owen, who walked off.

I pounded in the last of my stakes. "Sounds like he's not your usual helper."

My father dabbed his bald head with his handkerchief. "His younger brother often comes instead."

"You don't say." I flicked a pie tin and watched it twirl, glinting in the sun. "You put up these

tins to repel the birds. But you brought *him* here
to attract—me."

I glared across the garden at him, his sober
expression telling me I was right. He'd thought
he could anchor me here that way—and it struck
me that here was a third courtship, joining my
father's wooing of me and his being pursued by
his artist friend, Flora, in which one of the parties
had no wish to partake.

"You like playing God, don't you?" I asked
him. "You've got your vegetable Garden of Eden.
And we were to be your Adam and Eve."

He hammered in a stake without answering.

"Well then, I've got a prayer for you. Send one
of your angels unto Owen—and tell him that next
week he can stay home."

5

Epitaph

I brake the moment I see it. I look behind me, circle back, stop beside it, and get off my bike.

I crouch. There are ants all over its head. It's some kind of warbler. Or maybe a vireo. I'm no expert on birds, though I have progressed beyond my mother, who stopped at whippoorwills. Last fall I bought myself a bird book. And fell into the habit of taking a feather from those I find dead—which I do right now, carefully pulling one out from the tail. I hold it up. It's brown, edged with white. I thread it through the front of my cap. And at once I feel as if my hands aren't my own, as if someone else has willed this deed, and realize I'm taking part in a practice as old as mankind itself: identifying myself with an animal, in this case by wearing one of its feathers, hoping by doing so to acquire its characteristics, in this case swiftness.

I put on my cap and continue pedaling, unable to detect any gain in speed deriving from the feather. On the contrary, the new black pavement abruptly turns old and horrendously bumpy, slowing me down considerably. Each jolt travels up my arms and spine. I feel like I'm saving a trip to the chiropractor, the only silver lining I can think of. Peering around bends, I expect any moment that the road will regain its frosting-smooth surface. Half an hour later I'm still waiting, afraid I'll *need* to see a chiropractor, imagining nuts shaking loose from their bolts and the bike spontaneously disassembling. At last, the pavement improves—just a bit. As a connoisseur whose rock-hard tires convey every wrinkle in the road, I'm grateful.

I coast down a hill. I pass a beech tree and discover my thoughts turning back toward my father. I then cruise through the tiny village of Barbeau, whose downtown consists of an abandoned gas station. It dawns on me that the name is French, pointing my thoughts toward France, and toward Ben. I've been too busy in the week since graduation to miss him—but suddenly I do. I wonder how he's finding Paris and if there'll be a letter waiting in Maine. I calculate that we'll only have five weeks together back in Berkeley before heading off to our respective schools. Why, I ask myself sharply, didn't we think to apply to the same university? Then I recall applications were mailed in October, and that we didn't get to know each other until Christmas.

I ride beside a flower-filled meadow, my mind traveling a route of its own. Christmas. Ice skating. Ben skating backwards. France. Snails. Cave paintings. Van Gogh. My father's imaginary French baseball league. I pause on this last topic and find myself laughing at the strange silliness of his diversion. Then I remember that he operated this fictitious concern from October to April, and wonder if this was another of his subversions of mortality: a scheme yielding baseball year-round, creating a world of summer without end, a world in which winter never arrived.

To my right a hawk hovers above a field, hanging in the air like an asterisk, directing my eye to the grass below. I round a curve, lose sight of the scene, wonder about the hawk's hidden prey, and find myself daydreaming about mice. Which leads my mind to *Of Mice and Men*. Followed by musings on the turtle crossing the road in the opening of *The Grapes of Wrath*; the race between the tortoise and the hare; France, where I've read they eat rabbits, and horses; the Donner Party, stranded in the Sierras; then the current state of my own stomach—empty. I ride on a few miles, reach Greeley, population 672, pedal down the elm-lined main street, and decide to stop and eat lunch.

The town is larger than North Hooton, with two grocery stores to choose from. I stop at one, pay for a tin of sardines, some doughnuts, and an orange juice, and walk across the street to a park. Or "green," as they call them in this part of the country. I pass a statue honoring the town's Civil War dead, and eat under an elm. In whose shade I then stretch out, close my eyes—and next open them, to my utter amazement, half an hour later. I look at my watch, reach for my map, and find I've ridden twenty-eight miles. I'm nearly half done, and it's only 12:10. I can afford half an hour for a nap.

I pick up my stuff, ride two blocks, then take advantage of a gas station bathroom. Coming out,

I notice there's a narrow graveyard tucked between the gas station and a church. Knowing that I can spare the time, I prop the Raleigh against the low fence, open the squeaky gate, and enter.

The tombstones lean, as if tremendous gales have tormented the cemetery. A sparrow sings atop one of the stones. I stoop, peer at an epitaph, and make out "June 12th, 1828." The rest of the inscription is too worn to read. I move along to another gravestone, stoop again—and feel my eyes widen, at once recalling my Uncle Leo's visit to North Hooton when I see the words "Passenger, as you pass by . . ."

"... Remember you are born to die.
As you are now, so once was I.
As I am now, so you shall be.
Prepare for death, and follow me."

Leo's voice was large, like my father's, and he'd addressed this epitaph to the assemblage of tombstones as if he were a minister lecturing his flock. He turned toward me. "Preaching to the converted, I'm afraid."

I smiled in reply. I heard my father's ax in the distance and reread the inscription. "Remember you are born to die" was advice he'd certainly taken to heart. His death seemed to have cast its shadow over all his days—except for this one. When I'd come downstairs he was already up, zealously splitting wood, shouting to me that his heart would last a thousand years, fearlessly defying his demise.

"I'd forgotten about this little graveyard hidden away out here," said Leo.

I studied the inscriptions on a cluster of stones. "Most of their last names seem to be Pyle. And most of them didn't live very long."

"*Tempus fugit.* Time flees. A strong argument against sleeping in late." Leo stepped over the low stone wall. "Something a sluggard like me, with no wife or kids to wake him up, can use."

"You must not have slept too late to have driven all the way here from Boston by nine." I followed him over the wall and we continued our stroll through the woods behind the house.

"I got used to getting up early last semester. Had to teach an eight o'clock class." He converted a branch to a walking stick. "Italian literature of the Renaissance. A subject that put many students back to sleep."

We passed several gnarled apple trees, some bent-backed and dead, some with a few leaves, all looking misplaced among the pines.

"But tell me, Olivia—how are you finding rural

life?" A chipmunk darted past us. "Fresh eggs. Clean air. No bookstores for miles. Mosquito bites. Giant leeches in the lakes. . . ."

A woodpecker's drumming rang through the forest.

"It's all right," I replied. "Kind of boring, though." I searched for something more to say, then noticed Leo had halted and was pointing with his walking stick.

"Haven't seen that since I was a boy."

We both angled left and found ourselves approaching a large, stone-lined pit.

"What is it?" I asked.

The hole was about four feet deep and rectangular. "An old cellar, I suspect." He squatted at its edge. "Those rocks over there were probably part of the chimney—all that's left of the house."

I crouched. "When do you suppose it was lived in?" I realized I was speaking softly, as if we were intruding on its occupants.

"If those folks in the graveyard are the ones who built it, it might have been standing two hundred years back."

A chill skittered up the length of my spine. I stared ahead blankly. My ears heard no sound. Then I jumped down into the pit, my feet disappearing beneath a foot of dead leaves, and discovered my mind repeating a line that my teacher had paused upon when we'd read *King Lear* last year: "Ripeness is all." Walking around the basement, entranced, running my fingers over its stone sides, I knew that some bud inside me had burst. I no longer wanted simply to collect rocks; I wanted to know the lives of the people who shaped them into tools and lined their cellars with them. Buried lives, hidden like stones underground, waiting to be unearthed.

"They probably got their water from the creek over there." Leo gestured with his stick.

The house and its dwellers were becoming more real. The children had walked to the creek to fetch water, and no doubt had grown tired trudging up the hill. Their last name was Pyle. I thought back to the tombstones and tried to recall the first names I'd seen: Sarah, Nathaniel, Obadiah. Suddenly, I remembered something.

"Those apple trees—could that have been their orchard?"

"Good!" shouted Leo. "Why didn't I think of that?"

I broke into a smile, then reminded myself that my month of sampling my father and the fabled

East would be up in two days. By the time I'd climbed out of the cellar, explored the grounds, and found a rusty key, I wasn't sure I wanted to accept my option to rush right back to Berkeley.

"Sounds like your father's still splitting wood."

We emerged from the pines and could see him in the distance.

"Have you ever had any heart trouble?" I asked.

"Not a bit." A light breeze combed the long grass and played with Leo's wispy red hair. "The result, I believe, of a daily dose of Bluebird ale."

"Never heard of it."

"Good God!" he burst out in mock amazement. "Since I brought a six-pack, allow me to offer you your first taste—or would I be guilty of contributing to the good health of a minor?"

"What's the drinking age in New Hampshire?"

"No idea."

"My age exactly."

We greeted my father, still frantically swinging his ax like a wood-splitting John Henry. He'd brought out his radio and tuned in the Red Sox, which din we escaped by walking around to the front of the house and sitting on the porch, each with a Bluebird ale from the fridge.

"Smells like pea soup in the kitchen," said Leo.

He stretched his long legs and slowly propelled himself back and forth in his rocking chair.

"You know my father. He seems to think that pea soup is one of the four basic food groups." Having tasted beer only once before, I sipped cautiously from my bottle. Then I squinted, discreetly I hoped, and swallowed. "Something the body needs every day." I took a bigger sip, doubting I'd ever feel that way about Bluebird ale.

"Probably tied to his being a writer."

I scooted my chair toward Leo. "Why is that?"

"A lot of the greats in the arts lived on diets heavy in legumes," he declared.

I took another pull from my bottle, hoping that that might clarify matters.

"Tolstoy was a big pea-soup man. And then there was Schubert, dead at age thirty-one of an overdose of lentils. They say that near the end he'd trade away a song, a quartet, even an entire symphony for a pocketful."

My stomach was empty. I could feel the ale going to my head. In spite of which, I strongly suspected that this son of historians was making up facts, as my father enjoyed doing.

"Most scholars," he went on, "think that there

must be some special trace element in the beans."

"Vitamin Pea-Twelve?" I laughed at my own joke.

Leo belched and excused himself. "Some have even suggested a link between flatulence and the creative process."

I spit out my mouthful of ale, watering a potted geranium in the process.

"I've always been attracted to women who can hold their liquor, Olivia."

Upon hearing this, I spit out the swig I'd taken to replace the one I'd lost.

"However, despite your low marks on this point, I find you a most attractive niece."

All at once, I felt I might start crying. I stared at my uncle, flooded with gratitude. Why hadn't my father ever spoken those words?

"You ought to come down to Boston for a spell. I could drive you around, show you the sights. Take you to hear some good classical music."

"I'd love to. That really sounds wonderful." I took another sip from my bottle. "Though I have to admit that that kind of music makes me squirmy as a six-year-old." My father liked playing classical records, usually pieces with lots of singing, the sort that filled the entire house—and that made me want to head for the door. "All I remember from the one time I went to a concert like that is people coughing."

Leo rocked contentedly. "You'll find we have an extremely high quality of coughing down in Boston. Especially during the winter flu season."

I blew on my bottle, producing a breathy note, and assumed the connection between this act and the subject of music was clear. Leo blew two long steamship blasts in reply and I knew that our friendship was sealed.

"You've also got a great-uncle in Boston."

I gaped in astonishment. "I do?"

"Alexander Tomlinson Tate. He's in a nursing home, but his mind's still sharp as a needle. And his memory's stuffed full of tales of the merchant marine, campaigning for Roosevelt, fighting in the Spanish Civil War . . ."

My father. My uncle Leo. My great-uncle Alexander. And surely others. I suddenly had a sense of having come into a surprise inheritance of fascinating, unsuspected relatives, of being included in a wider family. A family I was pleased to find myself part of.

I finished my ale, my mind agreeably hazy. "The Big Dipper," I stated.

Leo looked baffled, and I realized that this time the connection wasn't clear.

"I feel like I've gone from a solitary star to part of a constellation," I elaborated.

Leo smiled at me. *"Benvenuta."*

I stared back at him, as puzzled as he'd been.

"Italian," he explained. "For 'welcome.' "

6

Jukebox

Columbus traveled by water, searching for land;
I'm doing the opposite. I recall from grade school
that he spotted a floating branch and felt sure he
was getting close. I pass a bait shop and feel the
same. Then I round a bend, pedal up a rise, and
behold the body of water I've been waiting for:
Lake Kiskadee, the farthest point on my father's
loop. I'm sweaty and tired. And despite the fact
I've been taking more rest and water stops lately,
I'm eager to celebrate reaching the lake with a
swim and a leisurely break from riding. Then I

71

remind myself that, like Columbus, I still have to make it back home.

I zip down a hill and pass through the little town of Fearnley, close to the shore. Keeping an eye out for a place to swim, I impulsively turn off the highway and onto a road running near the water. It's the middle of the week and many of the summer places I ride by are empty. I pass one dubbed "Dun Rovin." Then "Cabin in the Pines." Then I notice a stretch without any houses. I halt, walk my bike through the trees, and come upon a tiny cove. The view from the right is cut off by boulders. Up the shore to the left there's a cabin—windows shuttered and showing no signs of life. I climb down onto one of the ramplike slabs of granite rising out of the water. I unlace my shoes, then decide to take everything off, walk in to my waist, and dive.

It's late June but the water feels like February. I start doing the crawl, head away from the shore, and a few minutes later am comfortable, except for my scrapes, which sting a bit. I stop and tread water. The lake is vast—it would take me a week to swim across it. I spy a pair of sails in the distance, hear a few specks of sound from a beach, but can easily imagine I'm the only one here. It's quiet. The water laps against my neck. I enjoy the feeling of it surrounding my naked skin, and realize that I'd never swum without clothes before. There's something so different about it, and I sense that some part of me wanted to make this different from an everyday dip, to transform it into ritual. I think of baptism and of Mao's yearly swim across the Yangtze River. Then I wonder if my father swam here as well. I view the flickering images of my limbs. Am I, without knowing it, reenacting part of his annual rite?

My feet, dangling in the frigid water closer to the bottom, complain of the cold. Slowly, I make my way back to shore, clamber, dripping, onto my rock, and stretch out face-down in a patch of sun. I'm relaxed, cooled, utterly content. Then I hear the faint sound of a radio.

My eyes flick open. The sound becomes louder. Hurriedly, I get into my clothes, stand up, and catch sight of a boy, about ten years old, walking toward me through the trees. In one hand he's holding a fishing pole and a tackle box, in the other a radio. He notices me and veers to his left. I lie down again, watching him climb out onto a ledge overhanging the lake. He opens his box and baits his hook. He stands, and casts as far as he can. Then he sits down, gazing out at the water. I wonder what he's listening to on the radio, lift my head, and discover he's tuned to a baseball game. I make out the words "Boston Red Sox." And all of a sudden my mind begins entertaining the notion that this boy is in truth none other than my father. That people don't really die, but rather are assigned new lives different from their old ones, such that their families never recognize them. They become sugar-beet farmers in Idaho, or waitresses in Sydney, Australia. Or ten-year-old boys fishing on the shores of Lake Kiskadee, New Hampshire.

His hair is blond, as what little remained on my father's head was. His legs are long. I watch him kicking them back and forth and find myself wanting to talk with him. Amazed that I'm actually doing what I'm doing, I get to my feet, put my watch in the Raleigh's basket, and walk over his way.

I step onto a boulder lower than his and stare up at him. "Do you know the time?"

He looks at me and shakes his head. He's too young for watches, I realize. I know I should leave, but I'm not ready to yet. I want to hear the sound of his voice.

"Catching any fish?"

He shakes his head again. I need a different type of question.

"What kind of fish do they catch in this lake?"

"Bass," he answers matter-of-factly. "Bull-head. Sunfish. Chubsuckers . . ."

His voice is high and sweet—he could have stepped straight out of the Vienna Boys' Choir. I wonder if my father's was the same and study his face, searching for resemblances, trying to believe in my delusion.

"Who's winning the game?"

"Boston."

His tone doesn't disclose his loyalties. I'm about to ask if he's a Red Sox fan—than it dawns on me that if he isn't I'll have to surrender my fantasy.

"Good luck," I say instead. I linger a moment and smile, but he isn't looking—he's intent on his line, waiting for a bite.

I return to my bike, walk it to the road, and empty my canteen into my mouth. Watching for someplace I can refill it, I ride back to the highway and continue along the lake. The dent in my wheel is still scraping the brakes. My legs are reluctant to pedal. My back's tired. I wonder how my father managed, then remember that he was a cyclist in college. Knowing he'd jeer at my griping, I determine to complete the ride without complaint, and am instantly rewarded for this vow by the appearance of Jack's Lakeside Lounge.

I park by the door, take out my canteen, squeeze the water out of my braid, and step into the darkness within. I halt and wait for my eyes to adjust. They rise toward the dimly lit chandelier hanging above the bar, then pick out the glow from the tip of a cigarette hovering in midair beneath it.

"What can I do for you?" The cigarette moves.

"I was wondering if you'd fill my canteen." As if a fog is lifting in the room, I discern the shapes of two mountainous backs at the bar and a thick-necked man behind it.

"What do you want in it—whiskey or gin?"

One of the backs shakes with a chuckle, its owner turning to look me over.

"Just water, thanks." I hand over the canteen.

"How do you like it—straight, or maybe thinned down a bit with a shot of vodka?"

Another chuckle.

"Straight will do fine."

I expect him to ask me what brand I want, but he fills the canteen at a tiny sink and gives it back without any more jokes.

"Thanks." I turn, reach for the door—and just before opening it, glance to my right, glimpsing a man at an old-style jukebox, flipping through the plastic pages listing the names of the songs.

*　*　*

Mozart, *Requiem*. Bach, *Saint Matthew's Passion*. Beethoven, *Mass in C*.

Headlights moved across the wall. I straightened up and cocked my head. Not the sound of my father's ancient Plymouth Valiant. It passed the house and I returned to thumbing through his records.

Fauré, *Requiem*. Bach, *Cantatas 32 and 79*. Brahms, *A German Requiem*. You'd have thought he'd bought his collection from a funeral home going out of business. I wondered what he found in such music. The fantasy of a vast chorus of adoring mourners around his coffin? So much about him was a mystery.

I closed the record cabinet door, walked to a window, and gazed outside. Fireflies were flashing on and off between the house and the barn, their lights forming fleeting constellations. I stood and watched for several minutes, feeling strange having nothing more pressing to do than to look out the window at insects. Life with my mother was never like that. Trying to put myself to some use, I picked up the sack of butter-and-sugar corn that Owen had brought and put it in the fridge— next to the bag of string beans he'd brought the day before. Why did he bother bringing this stuff when he knew we had a garden of our own? Returning, I wandered about the living room, neatening shelves of books, blowing off dust, realizing how unmistakably manly its furnishings were: the photo of the 1946 Red Sox, the rodent skulls on the mantelpiece, the brass pipe holder, the fly fishing books, the *Sporting News* lying on the cluttered desk. Having never lived with males, I'd always thought them a mysterious breed, and now felt as if I were poking around a museum of masculinity, seeing close up how these strange creatures lived.

I meandered back toward the window and halted. Moths were thronging about the porch light, left on for my father, who was at his editor's weekend house fifty miles away. I hoped he was on his way home by now. Not that he was such charming company, but simply to have another person around. It seemed such a different house without him. I wondered if he felt similarly eager to return, knowing that someone would be waiting—then I viewed the room, and doubted it. It was the living room, but he'd made it his office: a desk where a couch should have been, file cabinets, a typing table, two chairs, his pump organ. Proof of his nonexistent social life, the work of a man who'd chosen isolation.

I looked at the phone, considered calling my mother, but resisted the temptation. I'd have felt obligated to tell my father about the call since it would show up on his bill, and though I didn't mind admitting that I missed my mother and thought about her a lot, I didn't want to give him the chance to crow that I couldn't take solitude.

I walked toward the case that held his own books, tilted my head, and scanned the titles. *Stark's First Case. Death on the Appalachian Trail. Death on Mt. Washington. Elegy for Virgil Stark. Murder at the MacDowell Colony.* I pulled this one out. The cover showed a hung man, his legs dangling beside a typewriter on a desk. I read the description on the inside of the jacket and found it dealt with a vicious literary critic found dead at an artists' retreat. Wishful thinking by my father, I suspected, and flipped through it, suddenly feeling guilty for never having read his books. On the other hand, he'd never read my grade-school stories, or my high-school term papers. I turned to his short biography at the back and saw that I was nowhere mentioned. Something, I knew, that shouldn't have surprised me—yet I felt disappointed. Flipping to the front, I realized that the book wasn't dedicated to anyone. I pulled out three others and found them the same. If it was true that no man is an island, my father was at least a peninsula.

I sat down with the book about the literary critic and had just begun reading when my father drove up. Not wanting to embarrass both of us by gratefully greeting him on the porch, I stayed seated and merely said "Hi" when he entered. He seemed ill-humored, didn't answer, and plopped his wallet and keys on the desk.

"How did it go with your editor?"

I watched him walk across the room, knowing exactly what he'd do next. While other adults had a drink when they came home, or sat in front of the television, my father relaxed by playing his pump organ.

"Terrific," he snapped. Sitting down before it, he worked the pedals to build up some pressure, pulled out a few stops, pushed in others, and spoke while he played something sad and slow from a beat-up book of Duke Ellington songs. "My editor is less than thrilled about the manuscript I just submitted. My publisher's verging on bankruptcy. And the accounting department's decided to let three more Virgil Stark books go out of print."

The organ seemed to be lamenting this news.

"What exactly does 'out of print' mean?"

My father looked peeved. "What it means is *dead*! No longer stocked and sold! Kaput!"

I searched for something consoling to say.

"Six titles dropped in the last two years!" In his agitation he pressed the pedals harder, raising the organ's volume and forcing him to speak even louder to be heard above it. "It's like having your garden ravaged by grasshoppers! Or seeing your children slain before your eyes!" He swayed back and forth on his stool while he played. "Parents, they say, should die before their children. Likewise, authors before their books. Something I thought I'd doubtless accomplish, given the condition of my heart."

I rolled my eyes. He flipped a page and returned to the beginning of the song.

"Maybe you should try something besides mysteries." I thought I'd made a helpful suggestion. When the music halted at once, I knew better.

"After twenty-one years, twelve short stories, and seventeen novels—*abandon* Virgil Stark?"

Instantly, I understood why he didn't subscribe to a newspaper. His poetry-loving detective was real to him; Virgil's latest case was his news. He was sustained by his artificial world, with no interest in the one reported in the papers, the one my mother and I tried to better. Were all artists, I wondered, so self-absorbed?

"*This* is the advice of the prospective heir whose duties would include continuing the series in my absence?"

"I withdraw the proposal." I could see I'd be better off changing the subject. "By the way, your friend Flora called while you were gone."

My father got up and took a pipe from his rack. "Friend!" He packed it with tobacco and lit it. "God save me from that woman's clutches. Something He could easily do, by making my next book a bestseller. One look at my name on the *New York Times* list and that pest, doomed to the failure she pretends to admire, would never speak to me again." He smiled at the thought.

"I put the note on your desk."

"With luck I won't find it. As you may have noticed, Neatness is only a very minor deity in my personal pantheon."

I viewed his desktop, covered to a depth of six inches with books, papers, note pads, and what looked like a month's worth of unopened mail. "The same," I remarked, "apparently goes for the god of prompt replies." I waved off a smoke cloud drifting my way.

"Mail improves with age, like wine. Something

your mother never understood. She couldn't let a letter sit for a day without answering it." He shook his head. "No doubt she spent a past life in debtors' prison, and determined this time around to be a creditor in every department— including that of correspondence. Always took pleasure in knowing the tides of mail were running in her direction. The Fundy Theory of Epistolary Behavior. No doubt she's written an article on it."

I crossed the room to dodge a fresh bank of smoke.

"Or perhaps," he went on, "she was attempting to single-handedly overload the postal system, hoping it would collapse and bring the government crashing down along with it."

"Better than single-handedly propping up the tobacco companies, as you're doing."

My father snorted and stared out at the fireflies. "If you haven't decided on a course of study in college, maybe you ought to consider a major in withering sarcasm."

Actually, I'd grown tired of such sniping. Searching for another change of topic, I picked up from his desk a piece of paper with "Bordeaux Bombers: 109-71" typed at the top. Below that was "Toulouse Guillotines: 104-76." I held the sheet out toward him. "What's this?"

He turned. "Final standings."

"Final standings of what?"

"This year's French baseball."

I considered his answer. "I didn't know that they played baseball in France."

He gazed back out the window. "You're right—they don't. It's my own private, winter league. Imaginary."

I looked down at the other teams on the list: the Arles Impressionists, Marseilles Escargots, Perpignan Red Sox, Avignon Popes . . .

"All the towns are in the south of France, where baseball could be played all year. I set up a schedule, then flip a ten-franc coin to decide who wins each day's games. Helps pass the time between October and April."

I puzzled over this odd amusement.

"My parents took Leo and me with them to France one summer," my father volunteered. He returned to the organ, fiddled with the stops, and began playing a light-hearted piece that sounded like it was coming from an accordion. He smiled. "Jesus, what a beautiful countryside! And what a terrific time we had. Eating a lifetime's worth of pastries. Gawking at the rabbits in the butcher shops. Amazing the locals with our baseball gloves. Have you ever been?"

"Not yet," I replied.

"We ought to think about going sometime." He glanced over his shoulder at me. "We had a farmhouse that year. Just outside of Arles. Maybe that's why I root for the Impressionists every winter."

"The Impressionists." I couldn't help but laugh at the notion. "At first base—Vincent van Gogh, I suppose."

"The team's leadoff hitter. Scrappy. Hot-tempered. Occasionally taunted by fans cutting off their ears and throwing them onto the field. Followed in the batting order by Pissarro."

"Then Gauguin."

"Right. Just brought up from the minor league club in Tahiti," my father declared above the music.

"And Renoir."

"Not much speed on the basepaths. But a good long ball hitter."

I tried to think of another French painter, wanting to prolong the game. "Monet?"

"Center field. Apt to study the grass out there and lose track of the score. Batting ahead of Toulouse-Lautrec."

"Known for drinking too much," I offered. "And for regularly missing the team bus."

He finished the piece he'd been playing and turned around on his stool toward me. "And for having the smallest strike zone in the league."

I winced. It was a terrible joke. But it was wonderful to find myself enjoying being with my father, for a change. "Would part of my job be to keep this league running?"

"It's really not much trouble," he replied.

"I suppose I'd need to start smoking too," I said in jest. "And playing the pump organ."

"Smoking is optional," he answered, apparently in all seriousness. "Though Virgil smokes a pipe, and it would be best that whoever continues the series knows a bit about pipes and tobacco. As it happens, he also plays the pump organ. A great fan of Duke Ellington's music, Virgil is. And extremely attached to the Mozart *Requiem*—a piece you'd need to know quite well."

He opened up his record cabinet. Knowing what was coming next, I said good night, climbed the stairs, and heard beneath me the sort of classical music I loathed and that Virgil no doubt loved. And knew that if I ever took over the series, I'd have to broaden his tastes.

7

Girl With Goat

First, I'm aware of the breeze picking up. Aspen leaves, which register the faintest movement of air, are trembling, causing the trees to shimmer like mirages.

Next, I notice the sky clouding over. The sun weakens. My shadow disappears, leaving me to ride on alone.

A few miles later I hear thunder far off. Shortly after that I glimpse lightning to my left. Pedaling past a lumber mill, I feel the first of the drops on my back.

No problem, I calmly inform myself. The paper called only for scattered showers. My shoulders can use a break from the sun. Some cool rain would feel great. And I'm riding on rubber, so there's no need to worry about electrocution. By the time I've finished delivering this glowing State of the Ride report, the wind is nearly blowing me backward, the rain is coming down like crazy, and I'm ready to consider selling my soul to the Devil for a room at a Motel 6.

Soaked, I reach a junction and stop. As if nothing could be more ordinary, I get off my bike, open my map, and, with sheets of rain sweeping over me, slowly figure out where I am. I turn onto Highway 520, headed south, pass a cow standing out in the downpour, and feel a sense of kinship with it. I consider holing up somewhere, but there's nothing but pasture on both sides of the road. Reminding myself of my sunset deadline, and feeling my father's eyes upon me, I decide to try to ride out the storm. I lower my cap, work my way up a monstrous hill, and find that I can't coast down it—as justice demands that I should—thanks to the wind blasting in my face. Indignantly, I press on the pedals, feeling like I'm riding through peanut butter, cursing out loud while knowing full well that it wouldn't have been safe to zip downhill, since my brakes aren't working in the blasted rain.

I push on, straining to see through the deluge, my wheels spraying me with water from below to add to that drumming on my back from above. A car passes, drenching me from the side, and I now feel a kinship with fish as well as cows. In movies, people begin laughing at this point, but I'm not Gene Kelly and this isn't *Singin' in the Rain*. Wondering what idiot wrote that film, I crest another hill and spot a steeple ahead. "Thank God!" I shout at the top of my voice. I've had it, and can't believe my father wouldn't have done what I intend to do: find someplace dry and wait out the storm.

I enter the town of New Glastonbury, and park in front of a cafe called The Nook. A sign reads "No shoes, No shirt, No service." Fortunately it doesn't say "No dripping." I shake my cap, wring out my braid, and glimpse my reflection just before I step in. I look as if I've swum ashore from a shipwreck, though no one inside comments on this fact. Grateful for Yankee reticence, I sit by the window, order a cup of tea, and watch the rain come down.

Two full hours and three tea bags later, I'm still watching—not only the rain, but the clock. It's now 5:10. I've lost precious time, and still have twenty-some miles to go. I'm dry now. The weather, however, is not. Showers are supposed to be short, but this seems more like the start of the forty days and nights. I hear my father's words in my head: "Our weather here in New England, Olivia, tends toward the apocalyptic. You'll find that forecasts often seem to have been lifted straight from Revelation." I peer through the window, thankful not to see fire and blood falling from the sky. Raindrops are proving trouble enough.

At the counter I buy a postcard of Mt. Washington, New Hampshire's highest point. Suspecting New Glastonbury is its wettest, I sit down and write to Ben in Paris.

"We can sure use the rain," I overhear a man say. I look up, annoyed, and feel like debating the point.

"Our alfalfa was about burnt up," replies the waitress. I watch her stop and refill the man's coffee cup, and for some reason—perhaps it's revenge—find myself imagining excavating the scene before me a thousand years in the future: the two of them represented only by a scattering of bones, a belt buckle, earrings; the wooden counter long rotted away; the plastic flowers in

the vase still in bloom; the coffee maker uncov-
ered intact, presumed to have been used in a
religious rite involving the teaspoons and cups
found nearby.

"Bad news, of course," the man declares, "for
that Republican Party picnic in Millbrook."

I feel a little better about the storm.

"Seems to be letting up," says the waitress.

I look out the window and find that she's right.
By the time I've finished writing to Ben, the sur-
faces of the puddles are still.

I pay my bill, mail the card at the post office
up the street, and ride on. I recall that the tale
of the tortoise and the hare crossed my mind several hours ago, at which time I'd no notion I'd
later be playing the part of the latter, struggling to catch up. Why, I accuse myself, did I
squander time on a nap—and on all those other
breaks?

Pedaling at a faster pace than before, I'm soon
out of town and surrounded by trees. The air is
heavy. Leaves are dripping. A thrush's song car-
ries through the woods. Except for the road I'm
riding on, there's no sign of human occupation.
In contrast, I picture bustling Berkeley, finding
it difficult to believe that I left it only yesterday.
I wonder what my mother is doing right now, if

the house feels empty to her—which I hope it doesn't, given I'll be going away to college in the fall. I miss her suddenly, and wish I'd chosen to go to school at home in Berkeley instead of moving down to Los Angeles. Coasting downhill through evergreens, my mind moves ahead, improvising imaginary scenes of college life. Then the trees recede, I pass a house in front of which a little girl is feeding some grass to a tethered goat—and at once I'm back at the county fair with Owen.

"Thirsty?"

I shook my head.

"What do you want to do next?"

"Just walk around, I guess." We'd already seen most of the sights: hundreds of pies, thousands of jars of preserves, the wood-splitting competition, rides, a country-western singer. During which I'd had time to consider my suspicion that my father was behind Owen's asking me—as well as his sporadic visits to the house. For although he'd stopped doing yardwork after that one occasion, he'd continued dropping by to pick up a few eggs, to exchange garden harvests, to study the phoebes nesting in our barn. He'd smile at me but not say too much, and seemed never to

notice or take offense to my saying even less in
return.

He bought a lemonade. "Livestock exhibit's just
up ahead."

"Might as well have a look." It was late August
and I'd grown used to being around him. And I
had to admit I'd been curious to see what a county
fair was all about. My father, I knew, wouldn't
have brought me. He hated noise and crowds.
And besides, when I'd come down for breakfast
he was already gone, having left a note saying
only "Back late."

We entered a barn and strolled past what seemed
like every known variety of chicken.

"Always have liked these Sebright bantams,"
Owen spoke up.

We stopped at their cage. I failed to find anything special about them.

"Graceful shape," he said. "Upturned tail."

The attraction of these features escaped me.
"I'm obviously walking with a poultry connoisseur."

He shrugged and smiled. "I just like drawing
birds." He flicked his dark hair out of his eyes.
"I carve 'em sometimes. The most beautiful ones."
He paused, seeming slightly embarrassed. "And
other things that hit me that way."

Surprised by this news, I followed him down the aisle. We graduated to geese, then moved on to ducks, guinea pigs, hamsters, rabbits, and stopped in front of the goats.

"Same kind you've got," Owen said, pointing.

I studied the animal, then found my attention drawn to the girl who appeared to have raised it. She looked about twelve, had a brown ponytail, and was busily sweeping out the pen. There but for the grace of divorce go I, I mused, watching her at work. I might have grown up a country girl and raised a goat each year for the fair, might even have been assigned to that pen. I gazed at her jeans and her gingham blouse, wondering if I would have dressed the same. She changed the water, then began brushing her animal. She seemed to know just what she was doing, and no doubt knew the arcane terms for all the parts of a goat. I hoped she'd win.

We walked on, turning up an aisle of sheep.

"Olivia!"

I spun around, wondering whether some other Olivia was being called.

"Right here, dear."

I turned toward the voice, and saw among the crowd of people strolling along my father's nemesis, Flora Gill.

She reached us. "And Owen. Enjoying the fair?"

Her shortness made me feel taller than ever. And her plumpness made me think of an overweight elf, carrying a folded parasol in place of a magic wand.

She grasped my arm. "Tell Bull that he's broken *all records* for canceling appointments to come and sit for his portrait."

"I'll do that," I said.

"And that I've made up my mind to paint it from memory. Seeing as I already know by heart every wrinkle and mole on that noble face."

She beamed at us. I wondered if she knew that she'd brought on some of those wrinkles herself.

"The eyes of the artist are always open," she declared. "The world always sitting for its portrait."

I noticed Owen smile faintly. And noticed myself distinctly relieved when, after a lecture in praise of the many anonymous early American portrait painters, little-known in their day but now regarded with the greatest esteem, we parted with Flora, then finished the tour of the barn and headed home in Owen's car.

We reached North Hooton, then Hatfield Road.

"How long until you go back to California?" he asked.

"I leave in three days."

He contemplated this answer.

"First I'll go to Boston for a week, to visit my uncle," I volunteered.

We rattled along, then swung up our driveway and stopped.

"Thanks a lot," I said.

Owen didn't answer, but opened the glove compartment instead, pulled out a small box, and handed it to me.

"What's this?" I asked.

He blushed. "It's for you."

I stared at it and blushed in return.

"Open it later."

I got out of the car and looked back at him. "Thanks—in advance. For whatever's inside."

I closed the door, watched him back down the driveway, then sat on the bottom porch step, inspecting the cardboard box in my hands. Had my father put him up to this as well? Figuring "later" meant anytime after he'd left, I undid the yellow ribbon, lifted off the box's lid, glimpsed something brown wrapped in tissue paper—then closed up the box.

I'd seen enough. It was something that Owen had carved from wood. What did it matter what it was if my father had prompted him to give it?

I wouldn't have put it past him, with his sole hope for a doting heir about to leave. He didn't want me to go without a memento he hoped would lure me back.

I took note of his car, still parked by the barn as it had been all day, then tried the front door. Locked, as I'd left it. I looked at my watch. 3:20. He must be taking a long walk. I'd put the matter to him when he returned.

I unlocked the door, put the gift in my room, then walked back out to the barn. I was no country girl, like the one at the fair, but I'd slowly befriended our goat, Josephine, and had taken over milking her, a chore I proceeded to tend to. After that, I harvested from the garden the makings of a giant salad—often all we ate in the evenings—and assembled it in the kitchen, for later. Then I poured some iced tea, picked up the book on the Iroquois I'd been reading over breakfast, moved out to the porch, and sat down in the rocker. Swallows were skimming the lawn, chattering. A phoebe was calling its name from a fencepost. Sounds that now seemed familiar, pleasant. And it struck me that I'd be leaving just as I was starting to feel more comfortable here. My sample month of Life with Father had passed, without comment, several weeks ago. Shortly before which, the energy that I'd formerly put into politics had finally found an outlet—in reading up on the Incas, Roanoke, Egypt: anything on vanished cultures I could find in my father's or North Hooton's library. Opening my book, and thankful that the mosquito population had dwindled, I read for the rest of the afternoon, until I was roused by a clicking sound.

I glanced to my left, closed my book, and stood up. He was shirtless. His face was flushed. Looking exhausted, with grease on one leg, my father pushed his bicycle up the dirt driveway and stopped before me.

"Plenty of time," he said, breathing heavily. He propped the bike up against the porch and sighted the sun. "Two hours at least!"

I leaned on the railing, watching him wipe the sweat from his head with a red bandana.

"Finished with time to spare!" he proclaimed.

"Finished what?"

He stretched himself out on the grass. "I'll tell you later."

Whatever the deed, I was glad to see that it plainly wasn't performed by a man afraid for his heart.

"Actually," I spoke up, "there's something I'd appreciate your telling me now." I came down the porch steps and stared at him. "Did you mention to Owen you'd be gone all day and that I might want to check out the county fair?"

My father sat up and eyed me in wonder.

"Was his giving me something your work as well? And his habit of dropping by the house?"

"What did he do to offend you now—open a barn door for you?"

"Just answer the question, please."

"The answer is *no!*" he bellowed, standing up. "The only thing I told him was *not* to come and do yardwork—as you insisted! Was I supposed to tell him to keep off my land too?"

We faced each other in silence, both startled: he by my accusations, I by the sudden conviction that he was telling the truth.

"That's all I wanted to know," I murmured. I walked inside, went up to my room, opened Owen's box, and unwrapped the tissue paper. And was amazed to find that he hadn't carved a bantam chicken or an eastern phoebe—but rather the right profile of my face.

I held the wooden silhouette toward the light. Each feature was true, every eyelash remembered. Dazed, I realized that he must have been studying my face during his visits. That, unlike me, he apparently found it attractive, even beautiful, worthy not simply of his sketchbook, but of wood. I thought back to the night I'd arrived and my hoping my father might compliment my looks, even if I'd known he was lying. Owen, I believed, was being truthful. And though I couldn't see losing my heart to him, I felt as if I'd always be grateful.

8

Sphinx Moths

Rounding a curve, I dodge a chipmunk, then spot the car ahead and have half a minute to decide what to do.

It's clearly a woman standing beside it, eyeing the tire. I glance at my watch. The highway's been mercifully free of hills for a while and I know I've been making good time. Surely I can spare a few minutes. Not that my father would, I feel sure. But that's not the side of him that I particularly want to emulate. My mother, I know, would stop without any such calculations, and I decide I'll stop too.

I slow down, coast, then put on the brakes, in the course of which approach I see that the car's an old convertible, that the left rear tire is flat, and that the driver is scarcely older than I am.

I halt beside her. "Need a hand?" I ask. I notice she doesn't seem thrilled to see me.

She gives me the once-over. "I've got a jack and all that," she replies. She looks up the road. "I thought I'd maybe get lucky and some cute guy would stop who'd know how to use it."

I'm stunned by her show of gratitude. So much for Good Samaritanship and Sisterhood Is Powerful. I'm ready to leave, my selfless concern for her welfare gone, then I find that it's been replaced by the desire to straighten her out. I get off my bike, bring down the kickstand, and vow to teach her how to change her own tire, just as my mother taught me.

"You'll need a lug wrench, a screwdriver, and a jack," I inform her. She's blond, attractive in her tank top and skirt—and looks as stunned as I'd been. She casts a last, sulky glance up the road, apparently figures she'll make do with me, and searches her glove compartment for a screwdriver. Something tells me it's not buried underneath books by Gloria Steinem.

I pry off the hubcap. She opens the trunk, finds the lug wrench, and we loosen the nuts. Then she gets out the jack and I put it in place.

"Now you use this rod and jack up the car."

She looks less than pleased at the prospect, but she does it. Under my prodding, she takes off the wheel, puts on the spare, tightens the nuts in the proper sequence, and lowers the jack. The whole chore is done in fifteen minutes.

"Guess I'll go on into town," she says.

She makes no move to kneel and kiss my running shoes, and I have the feeling I haven't changed her thinking a bit, much less opened the golden doors to a career in car repair.

"Thanks," she adds.

"No problem," I reply.

She takes off and I head down the road behind her. The sun is out and the highway dry. I ride along a lake for a while. The air smells of summer. The forests and fields are lush, so green with growing things that it's hard to believe this landscape will ever resemble a Christmas card scene. This summer day, similarly, has felt so long to me that it's seemed it would never become a summer night. But now, passing through a stand of birches, I see that the sun's dipped below the treetops and sense the coming on of evening. Tacking back and forth up the hill, I notice how long the shadows have grown and decide that, rather than sit back and coast down the other side, I'll shift gears and pedal. Which I do, the asphalt whizzing by beneath me and the air whistling in my ears. All of a sudden I glimpse a wing flapping to my left. I turn and gape. It's an owl! The first I've ever seen. Then just as suddenly, my handlebars jolt, in shock I discover I'm off the road, my heart somersaults, I reach for the brakes—and am halted instead by the trunk of a tree.

Adrenaline flashfloods through my veins. I find myself straddling the bar of the bike, my hands pressing against the tree as if warding off an attacker. This time, thankfully, I'm unhurt. Then I realize, to my terror, that my bicycle is not.

I get off, bend down, and inspect the front wheel. And see that it slammed into the tree near the dent it picked up earlier—and that the rim is now buckled hopelessly out of shape. I try turning it around but it won't pass between the brakes. I try bending it, then banging it with a rock I pick up, without success. I stare at it, and for some reason don't start swearing. There's no time for that. I need to concentrate on getting a new wheel—right now.

I look around. No houses in sight. And no time to go walking in search of one. I'll need to hitch-hike into the next town and hope that someone can fix me up there.

I haul the Raleigh over to the road and lay it down with its bad wheel sticking up. Despite which advertisement that I'm hitching out of need, not depravity, a woman in a station wagon zips by me. I gaze at the spot where I went off the asphalt. Hadn't I vowed, after the spill that morning, to keep my eyes on the road? That one was the fault of a truck and a pothole, but this one was all mine—unless you counted the owl. Even so, why should a few seconds' inattention be punished so severely, and just when I was near-ing home?

I hold out my thumb to a man in a truck, who eyes it as if he's checking for dirt under the nail and passes me by. At which point, my compo-sure begins to leave me and I feel like cursing him out. With no time to wait for some saint to come by, I decide that when the next car appears I'll wave my arms like a true damsel in distress. A minute later, a truck crests the hill. I get ready to flail—then notice a car slowing to a halt from the other direction. It's the girl I'd helped twenty minutes before.

Rejoicing to see her convertible, glad I played the Good Samaritan after all, I hurry across the road.

"I don't suppose there happens to be a bike shop in the next town," I ask.

She gawks at me. "In *Hopkinsville*?"

Suddenly, I wonder how I could actually have expected there would be—or that one would still be open at this hour.

"Any idea where I could get a new wheel?" Anxiously, I study the girl's face, hoping that I'll see it light up.

"Beats me," she says.

I peer into her eyes, willing her to think more deeply.

"Closest bike shop would probably be in Concord. Forty miles away."

"Too far," I reply.

She sighs, as if I'm asking too much, which I suppose I am.

"Around here, your only hope would be Lyle."

Her eyes don't light up, but mine do. "Who's that?"

"A junk seller. Down Wheelock Road. He's got everything under the sun—most of it rusted."

"Terrific! Can you give me a lift?"

She nods. I carry the Raleigh over, lower it into the back seat of her car, hop in the front, and we're off. I don't have to tell her I'm in a rush—she's quickly over the speed limit, zooming back the way I'd come, then turning onto a narrow road. The breeze in my face feels great, and though virtue may be its own reward, tangible compensation like a ride to a junk shop sure comes in handy. I think of my father, who wouldn't have helped with the girl's tire, or been helped in return. No wonder he worried about death so much: his unconnectedness to people left him without a vision of friends and family keeping his memory alive. My mother's house has always been full of people; I review my stay with my father and can't recall anyone coming to dinner.

"That's it on the right," my driver says.

I spot a ramshackle house ahead. I reflect on the fact that I've no doubt broken the rules of the ride by hitchhiking, then remember that if I get a wheel here I'll be having to ride about five extra miles—back to the place where I went off the road—and figure that that evens things out.

"That's his truck in the driveway." We pulled in behind it. "So he must be home. Mind if I leave you?"

At this, I rate my rescuer as only a fair-to-middling Samaritan.

"There's got to be a few bicycle wheels around here somewhere," she reassures me.

I scan the junk strewn about the yard and come to the conclusion she's probably right. If he doesn't have the size I need, I'll bet that there's another bike here that he'd let me ride home and bring back tomorrow.

I lift out the Raleigh. "Thanks for the ride."

"Anytime."

I wave as she roars down the road, lean the bike against a tree, then pick my way between lawnmowers, sinks, a mountain of hubcaps, assorted pitchforks and hoes, and finally reach the front door.

I knock. On the wall to my right is a sign saying "Lyle's Pre-Owned Merchandise." On the window to my left a bumper sticker reads "Ask me about Moore's Grease Remover." Deciding I'll pass up the invitation, I listen for footsteps, and don't hear any. I press the buzzerlike doorbell two times, peek around the side of the house, and behold a vast lot that seems to contain all the ingredients for a second Creation—most of the miscellany looking as if it's been sitting outside since the first one. Wondering if Lyle might be back there, wondering if he's here at all, I return, press the buzzer a full minute—and am surprised when the front door suddenly swings open.

"What in bloody blazes do you want?"

The man is gray-haired and stooped, but not, I perceive, the kindly codger type.

"I was hoping you'd have a bicycle wheel." I hear a voice from a radio within.

He looks peeved. " 'Trading Block' is on. Can't it wait?"

"Actually, it can't." I smile apologetically. "That's my bike up against the tree."

He sighs, stomps down the path, and inspects it. "How in hell did you manage that?"

I choose to regard the question as rhetorical. "I don't guess you could fix it."

"You guessed right," he snaps. "And some feller just bought up all but my little kid bikes. Don't think I've got that size wheel. Try Ray Meade in Essex." He straightens up and heads back toward the house.

"You don't *think* you've got it?" I catch up with him. "I'm a *customer*. Would you mind making sure?"

"You saying I don't know my stock?" he shouts. He stares at me and snorts. "I was in the pre-owned merchandise business *twenty years* before you started in dirtying diapers!"

"Look!" I shout back at him, angry and desperate. "I've got less than an hour to get back home! *Will you find me a Goddamn wheel or won't you?*"

He whips out a crescent wrench from his pocket, throws it down on the dirt, and storms off. "If you find one—it's yours!" He reaches the house. "Leave a dollar in the mailbox!" The door slams shut behind him.

I snatch up the tool and run to my bike. Using it to loosen the axle nuts, I take off the Raleigh's wheel and jog toward the back of the house with it. I pass through a land of lobster traps, then car engines, milk crates, shovels, screen doors. Turning up an aisle of junked cars, I climb onto the roof of a truck, look around, and spot a cluster of bicycles.

I dash over to them. They're all too little, and out of the question for riding. Then I notice a pile of parts nearby. Rooting through pedals, seats, handlebars, I spot a wheel, pull it out, and hold it up to the Raleigh's. Too small. Frantic, I scurry around searching for an adult bike that might have been missed. Nothing. I swear, and kick at a stone, which strikes a woodstove. I run toward it, climb on top, take another look around—and spot it an aisle away. Not a bike, but a handmade-looking cart, like the one my father used for compost and such, with what looks like a pair of bicycle wheels. I streak over, find that's just what they are, check one for size, and quickly remove it. The spokes have some rust, but it'll definitely do. Then I find that the tire is soft—and realize that that's actually good news. If the tire had a flat, there'd be no air at all. Rushing back to the pile of bike parts, I fish out a pump I remember seeing and hope that it works. It does.

Two minutes later, the new wheel's on the Raleigh. I put a dollar in the mailbox, place the wrench on top of it, get on my bike, and ride off. I didn't take time to look at the map—I know I've got about fifteen miles left. Nor did I peel my orange, the last of my food, even though my stomach's empty and I could use the extra energy. There's time for only one activity: pressing the pedals as hard as I can.

I reach the highway and retrace my route. The

sun, veiled by the trees, feels weak, and for once I wish it were back beating down on my shoulders from high overhead. As if keeping a death-watch, I'm constantly checking on it, noting each change in its condition. I recall that my paper, the *Concord Monitor*, said it would be setting at 8:30, and I wonder if that time's right for North Hooton. I decide that, the newspaper aside, if there's any sun showing when I reach the house, the terms of the ride will have been met. Then I picture the tree-covered hill to the west of the house, and pump even harder than before.

The roadside all seems vaguely familiar, a fifteen-minute *déjà vu*. Then I notice that the sensation has vanished and know that I've passed the site of my mishap. The memory of which locks my eyes on the road, which I read as a golfer does a green. I wind alongside a stream, cross a bridge. My palms feel numb from clenching the handlebars all day. My shoulders ache. My butt is sore, to put the matter mildly, and has grown to detest the Raleigh's rocklike seat. I lift myself off of it for a spell, and pass through Pittsford without breaking my rhythm—the last town before North Hooton.

I open up my canteen while riding, gulp down

some water, and pour the rest down my back. The sun may have lost its leverage, but the air's still steamy and my sweat glands have been working overtime. I'm on the home stretch. I check the sun, see that it's sinking, remind myself that I've got my father's long legs, and command my body to prove that I've got his cyclist's endurance as well.

I tear by a marsh, alarmed to find that frogs are already starting to croak. I cross the county line. I know I'm getting close and begin to search for signs of North Hooton. I pass the town dump at top speed. Then the windmill. I charge up a hill, my heart ready to burst. My eyes are sick of the sight of the road, legs shaky-weak, thoughts wild from exhaustion. *Why am I putting myself through this? I don't have to. I didn't even love him, for Christ's sake.* My lungs crave air, my chest feels close to caving in. I enter the town. *Because he was your Goddamn father, that's why.*

I pass the church, then the house with three chimneys, and turn by instinct onto Hatfield Road. I no doubt hear birds, dodge bumps, glimpse flowers, but my mind scarcely registers these events. The road turns to dirt. It's dim among the pines. I pass the Knotts'. Then the pond to my left. I spot the mailbox. Turn right, up the driveway. Run the bike up the hill toward the barn and look west.

And stare at the barest bit of orange showing above the hill.

I awaken the next morning, look at the window, and gaze at three panes of maple leaves, one of hillside, and four of sky. The sun, I notice, has risen out of view, and I realize I must have slept late. I reach for my watch and peer at the hands. 8:40. I have to be in town by 10:05 to catch the northbound bus, the first of three I'll need to take to get me to my dig in Maine. I get up, take my first step of the day, and wonder how I'll ever manage to take all the others down Hatfield Road.

I put on my clothes and creep downstairs. My leg muscles feel as stiff as beef jerky. My rear end's still sore. My shoulders and arms are bright red, having been well done by the sun. I eat breakfast on the porch, then, as if I'm climbing Mt. Everest, labor back up the stairs. I roll up my sleeping bag, strap it to my backpack, gather up toothbrush, cap, and comb. Taking a last look around the room, my eyes catch on the sight of the pair of sphinx moths mounted on the wall. I remember looking at them often last summer: at their amber wings, their blue-black eyespots, the label with their Latin and common names. Having read the Oedipus plays that year, I knew that the Sphinx was a creature who'd posed a riddle demanding self-understanding. I recall studying the moths my last morning and, as if they demanded the same of me, actually speaking aloud the words, "I'm not a copy of my mother." A statement that would have gladdened my father. I think of him, and of our parting that day.

"A great state, New Hampshire is," he said.

We both spotted the bus coming into North Hooton.

"Can five million chickadees be wrong?"

I smiled, leaned over, and picked up my suitcase.

"Oakes College, of course, is just up the road," he added.

"The third time you've told me today."

He paused. "As for my spot out on Hatfield, I don't think I'd be exaggerating if I said Thoreau would have sold his soul to IBM for the deed to the place."

I felt like I was being tempted to stay by Mephistopheles himself. "I'll try to visit sometime next summer." I looked at my father and at the now-familiar town behind him and suddenly knew that I really would try. "I promise."

This seemed to cheer him. The bus stopped before us.

"Then I'll keep your application for the position of heir on file," he said. The bus door opened. We didn't hug, but he patted my shoulder. I started up the steps. "And I want you to know, Olivia, that I think you've got what it takes. And that you've got the inside track for the job."

The door closed behind me and I moved down the aisle. It hit me that my father had never said anything quite like that before—and I felt as if I'd at last received the paternal blessing, something I'd been waiting for for so long.

Standing in front of the sphinx moths a year later, despite the recollection of that scene, and yesterday's tribute to my father, I know I'm not a copy of him either. That I'm not really the sort of heir he wanted. "I'm not a copy of either of my parents," I silently address the moths.

I look at my watch and know I'd better go. Slowly making my way downstairs, I feel like the Tin Man and can almost hear my legs creak with every step. I wash and dry my few breakfast dishes. I pull down the blinds. And on my way out, I grab the newspaper I bought yesterday. I lock the front door, padlock the barn, squeeze my fingers through the knothole, and hang the keys back up on their nail. I put on my pack and, heading down the driveway, flip through the paper until I reach the page with the sunrise and sunset times. And decide, as I turn up Hatfield Road, that I'll hold on to that particular page, which I proceed to tear out, fold up, and tuck in my pocket—the other half of my diploma.